"Marry me ... today."

Sheri's mouth dropped open. Could Manning be serious? "But we need a license and all that stuff. There's no way—"

Manning interrupted. "If I can find a way, will you marry me, Sheri?"

Elope . . . ? She hesitated. It would be totally out of character for her—she'd always been so organized, precise and *practical*.

"I love you, Sheri."

That was it. She didn't care whether things made sense. Manning Chandler loved her. She could see it in his eyes; she could hear it in his voice. "I love you, too."

"And you'll marry me? Now? I've waited a long time to find you, and I don't want to wait any longer. I don't want to give you a chance to change your mind."

"I'm not going to change my mind. I'll marry you anytime, anywhere."

Dear Reader,

When we first formed our writing team of Kate Denton a decade
ago, our goal was not simply to write a romance novel—but to
write a Harlequin Romance. We are thrilled to have reached that
goal and to be able to speak directly to the thousands of
Harlequin readers worldwide.

We're delighted, too, that our fifth book has been selected as part
of The Bridal Collection.

Love and marriage were a big part of our lives last year. While
working on this manuscript, each of us was also planning to be
mother of the bride. Carolyn's daughter, Leslie, married at the
historic Belo Mansion in our home city of Dallas, and Anne,
Jeanie's daughter, was married in Ecuador. Jeanie traveled to
South America to the site of a four-hundred-year-old hacienda
for the wedding (and in the process discovered a wonderful
setting for a future book).

Speaking of settings, northern New Mexico is a popular
honeymoon spot for Texas newlyweds and it's one of our favorite
places, too. We hope you'll enjoy visiting there as you read Sheri
and Manning's story as they promise *To Love and Protect*.

Sincerely,

Carolyn Hake and *Jeanie Lambright*
(Kate Denton)

TO LOVE
AND PROTECT
Kate Denton

Harlequin Books

TORONTO • NEW YORK • LONDON
AMSTERDAM • PARIS • SYDNEY • HAMBURG
STOCKHOLM • ATHENS • TOKYO • MILAN
MADRID • WARSAW • BUDAPEST • AUCKLAND

ISBN 0-373-03223-4

Harlequin Romance first edition October 1992

TO LOVE AND PROTECT

CHAPTER ONE

"So someone's threatening to kill Manning Chandler. Well, I'm not sure I blame him." Sheri glanced at the report spread out in front of her. The report on Wallace Security's newest client.

"Me, neither," Tom Wallace agreed. "I've got a good mind to pull our agents out of there. The only thing that's stopping me is the fear of offending his father. Chandler Oil puts a lot of money in our coffers." Tom fed some coins into the drink machine, pushed the button for a cola, then turned back to Sheri. "We're probably in trouble, anyway. Young Chandler makes no secret of the fact that he views us as a bunch of incompetents. A client like this one makes me rue the day we left the Houston Police Department." He retrieved his soda and joined Sheri at the table.

"You may regret leaving the streets, but I sure don't," Doug Wallace announced as he entered the break room. "Have you forgotten what it was like? Teenagers tossing rocks at cars, neighbors mowing the lawn too early in the morning, dogs barking. More baby-sitting and nuisance calls than anything else. It sure wasn't 'Miami Vice' reruns with officers in designer clothes chasing bad guys in fancy sports cars."

Tom pulled a hamburger and fries from the take-out sack and unwrapped them. "You're on target there, and no, I haven't forgotten. Take the time I was a rookie—fresh out of the police academy. I spent the whole afternoon rounding up chickens on the freeway after a traffic accident. Four years in college, *plus* academy training, and there I was chasing chickens."

Sheri cleared her throat. She'd heard the story at least a hundred times; it was one of her oldest half brother's favorites. "Let's get back to the matter at hand—Manning Chandler, remember?" She straightened the pages of the file, arranging them neatly in front of her.

"Relax, little sister," Doug admonished. "Everything's under control. I'm flying out there tomorrow to smooth Chandler's ruffled feathers and to beef up our investigation. So what's next on the agenda? And who's got quarters for the machine?"

Sheri sighed as Tom fished around in his pockets for change. The break room was an unlikely site for a weekly business meeting, but it served as neutral territory. Her business-partner brothers chafed at gathering in Sheri's neat-as-a-pin, everything-in-its-place office, while she resisted meeting in either of theirs, which she—generously, she thought—referred to as "pigsties no self-respecting pigs would live in."

It was amazing the three could operate a business together, since their working styles contrasted as much as their offices. Tom and Doug were easygoing, Sheri more intense. Frequently there were clashes of wills, which usually ended with one of the men telling Sheri to "lighten up."

Perhaps she *was* too serious on occasion, but hard work and proving herself had been necessary most of her life, and it was difficult to change ingrained behavior. "We'll get to the rest of the agenda in a minute," she said. "But I'm not through with Chandler."

Doug groaned. "Pay attention, Sheri. I said I had everything under control. First thing in the morning I'm off to that New Mexico resort of his." He got a soda from the drink machine, then sat down at the table, grabbing one of his brother's french fries and popping it into his mouth. "Any more burgers in that bag, Tom?"

"Keep your hands to yourself, little brother." Tom moved the sack out of Doug's reach. "This is my lunch, not a grazing site for you." All of a sudden, the men were arguing as if they were ten and twelve again, rather than in their thirties.

Sheri was determined to wait out this distraction, feeling more like their mother than their youngest sibling. Most of the staff meetings followed the same pattern. Serious discussion, then at some point, a skirmish between the two "boys." But for all the seeming disorganization, the partnership worked.

"The Three Musketeers." That's what the trio had dubbed themselves one evening at Sheri's apartment after deciding to resign their jobs as Houston police officers and start their own security and investigation firm. The business, Wallace Security, was barely three years old but it was flourishing, with branch offices in Oklahoma City and Albuquerque. Everything had been going better than anticipated. Everything, that is, until Manning Chandler IV signed on as a client.

Chandler had hired them because of some anonymous notes warning him that his life was in danger. Their assignment had seemed straightforward enough: provide extra protection, while trying to find out who was responsible for the notes. But what had initially appeared simple had become anything but.

The Wallaces soon discovered their firm was a replacement for another one, a big-name national company that had failed to do the job. So even though he'd sought them out, Chandler had already formed a negative opinion about security companies in general.

Since the first day they'd been hearing a litany of complaints—from their client and from their agents. Nobody involved with the project had a good word to say about it.

Chandler had been no stranger to Tom and Doug; he'd met her brothers when the business was just beginning to grow. While Sheri was establishing the first branch office in Oklahoma City, they were negotiating with Chandler Oil to provide security for its highrise complex in Houston. At the time, Manning was with his father's firm, and the Wallaces had formed a nodding acquaintance with him. Apparently their work had been professional enough to make him remember the company after he'd fired their predecessor. But it didn't protect them from the doubts already lodged in Manning's brain.

"I think I should take this one," Sheri finally said.

"Get serious, sis," Doug countered. "You've read his file. I doubt you, or any woman for that matter, could please this particular client."

Sheri rose to her feet. "What? I most certainly—" Then she caught herself. When she was younger, she'd given her fiery temper free rein but had since realized that such outbursts were unproductive. No need to overreact to her brother's goading. "Keep in mind," she said coolly, using her fingers to emphasize each point, "that, one, I'm in top-notch physical condition. Two, I can shoot as well or better than any agent in the firm—including either of you. And three, and most important, I worked in homicide investigations for more than a year before leaving the department." Sheri picked up the scheduling calendar. "Besides, Doug, you're supposed to go to Galveston regarding those cruise-ship robberies."

"Someone else can handle that for Doug," Tom said. "He's better suited for New Mexico. After all, this isn't typical duty. As the file indicates, the job has put several of our agents out of commission. Our client complains it's because the people we've sent are inept. But according to the agents, Manning Chandler is a pain in the kazoo, and working for him is like a course in survival warfare. With all the injured agents we've had to replace, we could almost install a revolving door at our office there. Bottom line is we have a very unhappy customer. The only thing that's kept him from kicking us out on our duffs is the six-month contract he signed. We don't want you in that kind of situation."

"Cut the protective big-brother stuff," Sheri said. "I can take care of myself, and the two of you know it." She leaned on her hands and glared at each of them in turn. "I thought we'd laid that to rest years ago when I beat down your objections to my entering law enforcement. Since then I've been in plenty of dangerous situations. As a matter of fact, this seems a lot safer than the divorce case I just finished."

"It's not just that," Doug said. "You're overlooking the guy's playboy reputation. Remember all those newspaper articles when he still lived in Houston?"

"Yes, and now that I think back, I recall how they reminded me of you." Sheri laughed. The colorful escapades of the son of Texas billionaire Manning Chandler III were really nothing too outrageous. Lots of parties, lots of women—usually a debutante or Hollywood starlet on his arm—and frequent society-page rumors about new romances or speculations about forthcoming engagements.

She sat back down and eyed Doug. "On reflection, I definitely think I have to take this assignment. Sending you to a spa in Santa Fe would be like sending Brer Rabbit to the Briar Patch."

"I'm wounded." Doug dramatically clutched his chest. "No one will take me seriously until I'm an old married man."

"Drop the theatrics," Sheri said. "You're needed in Galveston, and I'm the logical one to go to New Mexico. Case closed."

"Okay, if you insist on taking this gig, then go for it. Just make sure you don't get too involved with our client. He's left a trail of broken hearts from here to Santa Fe."

Sheri smiled at her brother. "Not to worry, Douglas. Dealing with a self-styled Casanova like Chandler ought to be a cakewalk after a lifetime with you and Tom. Now, let's get back to the agenda.'' She read off the next item and the partners' meeting continued.

SHERI PULLED a folder from her briefcase as the plane began its taxi onto the runway. She'd had a restless night thinking about the job ahead of her. As confident as she might feel about her investigative skills, Doug's cautions about their client's much publicized liaisons with women had struck a nerve. Sheri didn't have a lot of experience in male-female relationships. Maybe she was taking on more than she'd bargained for.

The folder containing a variety of materials on Manning Chandler IV only succeeded in adding to her doubts, taunting her with an article about Manning Chandler and Fort Tranquillity, his popular fitness and outdoor-adventure center near Santa Fe. The elite spa was multipurpose, its visitors ranging from serious physical fitness buffs to celebrities seeking rest and recreation.

Sheri flipped to a publicity photograph showing their client in his gym, surrounded by body-building equipment and healthy-looking, curvaceous women in tights and leotards.

Even though she'd never met Manning, Sheri was familiar with his father, Manning III, or Trey as he was called, having spotted him a time or two at Chandler Oil. The elder Chandler was a handsome man, tall and trim, with patrician good looks, but he couldn't hold a candle to his son, a blond Adonis dressed in gym shorts and a T-shirt. Nice legs, Sheri mused, then wondered why such a thought had entered her mind. She turned to the next picture, a full-page head shot. His eyes—a rich lapis blue—were fringed with pale eyelashes and framed by heavy blond brows. His nose was slightly aquiline, his cheekbones high and strongly defined. His mouth ... well, sensuous was the only appropriate word.

Sheri had seen pictures of him before, but she'd never paid much attention. To be fair, she had to admit that Manning Chandler IV was definitely the kind of man females looked at twice. At *least* twice. The kind of man most women found impossible to ignore. But then, Sheri wasn't like most women. Since her teens she'd been determined to be her own person, free from dependence on a man. She'd seen more than enough of the clinging-vine routine with her own mother; she intended to avoid making the same mistake.

The plane landed on schedule. Anson Bruce, director of the Albuquerque office, was waiting for her at the luggage carousel. After a brief stop at the branch office for introductions to the staff and a tour of the facilities, the two departed in Anson's Mercury sedan for Santa Fe, some sixty miles north.

"You had time to study the file?"

Sheri nodded. "Pretty much. From what I understand, there's nothing new on the threat. Just a couple of notes telling Manning Chandler to beware, implying that he's going to have an unfortunate accident."

"That's about it. Of course, the only people who've had any accidents so far are the Wallace Security agents," Anson lowered the car window and rested his elbow on the ledge. "Mind? I like the fresh air."

"Not at all," Sheri said. "It smells wonderful. So clean and crisp. It's nothing like Houston."

"You may find that the only advantage of being out here." He reached into his pocket for a roll of antacid mints, offering one to Sheri before flicking a couple into his mouth. "Frankly I'm glad the brass decided to take over. I'd just as soon eat a bushel of jalapeños as put up with Chandler."

"Surely he's not that bad." Judging by everything she'd read, he *was,* but there was no point in starting off the assignment by criticizing a client in front of an employee. Besides, maybe Chandler's bad-boy reputation had been exaggerated.

Anson's eyebrows almost merged with his hairline. A vein throbbed in his temple. "Oh, no? Not that bad? I can't recall a more uncooperative client. You'd think we'd forced our way into his private domain, instead of being there at his behest. When we suggest he curtail his activities until we get to the bottom of this, he treats the suggestion like a dare and does just the opposite.

"Three agents! Three agents he's put out of commission in as many weeks. First, Munoz with the worst case of poison ivy I've ever seen, then O'Donald's broken leg. And now, Pete Garcia has a dislocated shoulder."

So much for the exaggeration theory, Sheri thought.

Anson went on. "Chandler gallivants all over the countryside, subjecting everybody to a physical regimen that makes military boot camp seem like a romp in the park. It's taken its toll. And left our client totally disenchanted with Wallace. Tom tells me there may be a chance of losing the contract."

"It's a possibility."

Anson merely shook his head in reply, the resignation in his expression causing Sheri more concern than his earlier tirade.

They exited Interstate 25 and entered the city limits of Santa Fe. The trademark buildings gave the town a distinctive postcard appearance. "Ever been here before?" Anson asked.

"No. I wish we had time for a little sight-seeing."

"I'm afraid you'll have to take a rain check. We're going to be late if we don't drive directly there." He wound through the narrow streets, then sped into the hills toward Fort Tranquillity.

"This guy certainly seems to have adequate protection." Sheri looked around as they sat in the car outside the guard station while the attendant inspected their credentials. When he'd finished, the guard went into the small house to use the phone, then waved them on, a high wooden gate swinging open to permit passage.

"Is this the equipment we installed?" she asked.

"Yep," Anson said. "The place is probably better fortified than the Pentagon now. Chandler's also got his own security staff. He continually reminds us that our agents are to focus on the investigation, provide a little extra insurance, and *not* worry about day-to-day security. I wish he'd concentrate on the spa and let us do our jobs, instead of second-guessing us all the time."

Anson gestured toward an imposing adobe mansion. "There's your temporary home." The house, part of a vast complex, sat atop a rugged hill, ringed by athletic facilities and various forms of housing, ranging from cabanas to a dorm. One of the Wallace employees was coming through a pair of huge, intricately carved double doors as they turned into the circular driveway. He waited while Anson and Sheri pulled up to where he stood.

Anson introduced her to Pete Garcia. The handsome agent's right arm was in a sling, and his shoulder was taped beneath his cotton-knit shirt.

He reached out his left hand. "A pleasure, Sheri. Glad you're taking part in this operation." Pete's words were gracious, but he had an expression of incredulity in his eyes. "I have to confess I'm surprised my replacement is a woman," he admitted. "Even if she is one of the bosses."

Sheri knew Pete's expression said more than his words. She'd seen it before when arriving for an assignment. She smiled to herself—she might not look the part of a bodyguard or private investigator, but appearance wasn't a job qualification. In fact, she felt her looks gave her an edge in working undercover.

"Come on in and meet Chandler," Pete said. "I think Agent Lightfoot's with him now."

Inside they were joined by a tanned muscular staff member dressed in tank top and shorts. He introduced himself as Juan, Manning Chandler's personal assistant, and led them to the rear of the house, where Chandler's large office overlooked an Olympic-size swimming pool.

Manning Chandler IV was perched on the corner of a large mahogany desk, talking on the phone. He was facing the pool and seemed oblivious to the audience hovering at the door.

From his side of the conversation, it was obvious he was talking to one of her brothers, probably Tom. It was just as obvious that Tom was being conciliatory, altogether *too* conciliatory. Sheri was unable to quell her annoyance. Diplomacy was one thing, kowtowing another. She realized customers were the lifeblood of every business, but she didn't subscribe totally to the adage that the customer was always right—especially this particular customer.

After completing her review of their files on Manning Chandler, she'd developed a negative impression of him. A rich man's son, he'd grown up with every advantage and apparently frittered many of them away, including a future as the CEO of Chandler Oil. She had to be objective if she wanted to get to the bottom of the threats, as well as investigate his complaints about Wallace Security. But reading the reports, she'd surmised that the man was spoiled and arrogant and probably enjoyed putting fresh agents through the grinder. It was unfortunate that Tom hadn't chosen to be more forceful with him. Apparently she'd have to be the one to rein in this recalcitrant client.

"I don't want you sending some macho hotshot who's looking to prove himself, Wallace," Chandler warned. "These threats have to be kept quiet." He ran his fingers through his hair. "My business would go down the drain if my guests didn't feel they were safe.

Not to mention the fact that this kind of notoriety could give every other kook in the country similar ideas. So, no hero types, okay?'' As Chandler continued in the same vein, Sheri wondered what was going on at the other end of the telephone line.

Was her brother intimidated by Chandler, and if so, why? It wasn't his usual nature. Tom might be too agreeable occasionally, but he wasn't easily intimidated. Sheri had always thought her oldest brother couldn't be ruffled by man or beast. Why, then, hadn't he told Chandler that "macho" wasn't an appropriate adjective in this case? Was Tom indulging in a bit of harmless amusement at his client's expense? Probably. Her lips curved in a hint of a smile. Manning Chandler was in for a surprise.

Anson cleared his throat, drawing Manning's attention. "I'll get back to you, Wallace," he said, hanging up the phone and scowling in the direction of the agents standing in the doorway. Sheri studied him as he glanced from Anson to Pete Garcia to Frank Lightfoot—who'd just come in—and finally to her.

He was as handsome in person as his pictures had promised, but his blond hair was slightly tousled and his deep blue eyes were wary. He looked at Anson again and shook his head. "Not you, Anson. Give me a break. If these young bucks can't keep up with the pace, how do you think a veteran like you will manage? Especially one whose major food source is antacids.''

"Sorry to disappoint you," Sheri interjected, "but I'll be replacing Pete. Sheri Lindsey, Mr. Chandler.''

As Manning turned his attention to her, she walked over to shake his hand.

His thick brows arched as his eyes widened, his expression suggesting that she'd taken leave of her senses. The eyes, now slightly hostile, undertook a quick survey, beginning with her shoulder-length russet hair and chocolate-brown eyes. Then they scanned her curvaceous frame, scrutinizing her in the same careful manner a scientist might view a laboratory specimen. In the quiet of the room, she could almost hear eyes blinking.

Sheri felt her face heat, her defenses hitting full alert in anticipation of what was coming next. She'd heard *all* the hackneyed comments before: "Doll, you look more like a Hollywood starlet than a security agent," or, "A cupcake like you is going to handle our investigation?" or, the worst one, as far as Sheri was concerned, "Honey, I'd *love* having you guard *my* body." Which one would this…this cretin use? She was ready to launch a bristling retort when Manning spoke.

"Ms. Lindsey. Welcome to the Fort." His voice was coldly polite. "I assume you're here because you can do the job?"

In the face of his patronizing question, Sheri found herself more annoyed than ever. She was a trained agent and one-third owner of Wallace Security, another fact her brother had obviously omitted during their telephone conversation. Oh, well, she didn't need Tom running interference for her. "Mr. Chandler," she began, smiling sweetly, "I assure you I wouldn't be here if I couldn't do the job. I'm not only a qualified agent, but also a partner in Wallace Security. So, if by some quirk of fate I can't handle it, I promise the company will call in a big strong man to take over. Or, if you'd prefer, the National Guard.''

He grinned slyly but made no comment, obviously amused by her response. The only thing missing from the scenario were the unsaid words, ''You're cute when you're angry.'' Sheri would have liked nothing better than to eradicate that smug expression with a few select phrases borrowed from her days on the beat, but refrained; after all, this was her livelihood.

Be professional, she told herself, taking a deep breath. *Calm down. You can't let him get to you in the first five minutes.* She looked evenly at him, trying to restore her equilibrium and ignore the irritating twinkle in his eyes. ''Now that we've been introduced, Anson and Pete need to drive back to Albuquerque. But before they go, I'd like a briefing from them. Can we meet later—say, in half an hour—to discuss what's been happening and how I can work with you?''

''Okay by me,'' he answered with little enthusiasm. ''I'll buzz you when I get off the phone. I'm expecting a call from the West Coast.''

The agents left Chandler's office and spent the next quarter hour hunched over the desk in the command room. ''Chandler received another threat this morning,'' Frank said. ''Same modus operandi—a brief typed warning to watch his step.''

''Not much to go on,'' Anson muttered. ''Got anything else?''

''Nah. It's impossible to come up with any information. Chandler gets bent out of shape if we suggest talking to the guests.''

"No wonder the last group failed," Sheri said. "He's really tying our hands."

"You're right, but he keeps telling us that he doesn't want a big production—and he refuses to call in the police. His greatest fear seems to be publicity. The staff knows why we're here, but the guests don't. That's why he won't hear of a full contingent, just a couple of inconspicuous agents. 'Blend in with the scenery,' he says. I guess we're supposed to gather information by osmosis."

Frank walked Anson and Pete to the car, then rejoined Sheri in the command office while she waited for her meeting with Chandler. Despite Frank's cordiality, Sheri sensed the agent wasn't comfortable about having a woman as a partner.

His next words confirmed her suspicion. "I don't know if anyone explained, but this is not your typical protection scene."

"No, we don't usually have to deal with an actual threat of violence," Sheri answered, being deliberately obtuse.

"That's a concern, but it's really not what I meant." He rubbed the back of his neck. "Uh ... this may get me fired—it's hardly the comment an employee should make to a lady boss in this day and age, but this job's not right for a woman."

As outdated as his message was, Sheri felt almost sorry for Frank. He *was* trying to be tactful. He wasn't succeeding, yet she had to give him points for effort.

"Three weeks here, and I've aged ten years," he complained.

"I've gathered that Fort Tranquillity is a misnomer," Sheri said, hoping that open conversation would increase Frank's confidence in her. Mutual respect was essential in this business. He had to feel his partner could handle her end of the job. "How did Chandler come up with the name?"

"From what I hear, he's a fan of old Western movies, so he wanted to call the place Fort something-or-other. He's also got friends in Houston who are involved in the space program—remember Tranquillity Base from the moon landing? Anyway, he put the two together. Personally I think Fort Massacre or Fort Defiance would be better monikers." Frank shook his head. "The only time we get any rest is when one of Chandler's groupies is on the scene. And, thank goodness for small favors, there are plenty of them, so they occasionally manage to keep him occupied.

"I don't think the guy's intentionally out to do us in," Frank went on. "He just won't settle down and he's gung ho on the fitness thing, which means the net result is the same. I thought I'd trained to be a cop, not a marine. Maybe one of those guys could tolerate the pace—rock climbing, twenty-mile hikes, wilderness survival—but I hate it. And you, well, just call me sexist, but like I said, this really isn't a job for a woman."

"Thanks for the warning," Sheri answered unemotionally, suppressing the urge to respond to his latest remark with a verbal broadside. Her patience was definitely waning. If Wallace Security hadn't been running short of agents for this assignment and already in danger of jeopardizing their contract, she would reassign Frank elsewhere. But at the moment she needed him. She found the thought depressing.

Like many other males before him, Frank was falling victim to judging on appearances. He had no way of knowing that Sheri relentlessly pursued various forms of exercise. Her strenuous workouts served more than one purpose. Not only did they keep her conditioned, they also enabled her to burn off excess energy.

Running was her favorite activity. She'd been a track star in high school and had dreamed of the Olympics until her once boyish figure had developed curves more useful for beauty contents than competitive sports. Still, she'd remained committed to total physical fitness.

Frank broke into Sheri's musing as he continued his briefing. "The next thing he's got planned is a white-water rafting trip. Sounds like it should be fun, but I can promise you it won't be. Chandler seems determined to make everything a challenge. I'm not sure the guy knows how to have a good time. I mean, just relax and enjoy himself."

Sheri missed the end of Frank's comment, having frozen at the mention of "white-water rafting." It was her deep dark secret. Even though she was an excellent swimmer and a qualified lifeguard, she was actually terrified of water, especially moving water. She wasn't certain about the origin of this phobia, but figured it might be tied to the time she'd fallen off a dock in Port Aransas when she was a toddler. She didn't remember the incident, but Tom and Doug had told her about it. Whatever the reason, she'd been unable to overcome the fear.

The intercom rang. "Thanks for the background, Frank. I think Mr. Chandler's ready to see me now." Sheri almost expected Frank to follow her. If so, she'd just have to be firm. She was in charge here and could handle the client alone. But Frank didn't move. His concern notwithstanding, he obviously understood company protocol.

Manning Chandler was pacing back and forth across the Navajo rug on the floor of his office when she entered. "I'm starting to have some doubts about this."

"You mean you object to my being a female?"

"On the contrary, it's the only possible gender with a body like yours." His eyes were appraising.

"Mr. Chandler—"

He raised his hands in silent apology. "Really, Ms. Lindsey—Sheri—it takes someone in excellent condition to keep up with me."

Probably in more ways than one, Sheri told herself. She stopped. Chandler was talking about his business. Why had her thoughts suddenly strayed in other directions? She returned her attention to the subject at hand. "Why don't we see how it goes?" she suggested in her calmest, most professional voice, giving him a tight little smile. She wasn't about to quit simply because a couple of nineteenth-century men had decided she wasn't up to the job.

Manning's cunning smile matched her own. "Perhaps you're right. I should wait and see. Just to prove I'm not as unreasonable as they say I am."

Sheri started to respond, but Manning went on before she could speak. "Don't worry about denying it. I've heard the scuttlebutt—'hard-nosed,' 'domineering,' 'impossible to work for.' Funny, I have a whole staff who appear to have no complaints. And yet to Wallace Security, I'm a combination of Simon Legree and Attila the Hun. Frankly, I think it's the excuse of incompetents. However, I'm willing to give Wallace one last chance. Not that the contract appears to be too important to them. I was led to believe Doug Wallace would be handling this personally. Instead—"

"Instead," Sheri interjected smoothly, "the third member of the management team is handling it. As someone with a vested interest, I can assure you the contract is very important to us."

"I suppose that, *and* what kind of agent you are, remains to be seen." Manning paused for a moment, apparently waiting for her reaction. If so, he was going to be disappointed. Annoyed as she might be by his attitude, a defensive recitation of her credentials would accomplish nothing at this point.

When she failed to respond, Manning continued, "But remember, I don't have unlimited patience."

From what I've heard, you have no patience whatsoever, Sheri wanted to reply. Again diplomacy took over. "I can deal with a bit of impatience," she said. "All I ask is a fair opportunity to do the job."

CHAPTER TWO

IT WAS ALMOST MIDNIGHT. Sheri was sitting in the office assigned to Wallace Security, reading a mystery novel—or trying to. Her mind kept wandering back to the events of the day. She was still irked by the less-than-enthusiastic welcome she'd received. She should have anticipated a negative reaction; it had happened before and undoubtedly would again. Despite a multitude of novels and television shows about female private investigators and police officers, many people held on to the antiquated notion of law enforcement and security services as male-only clubs.

Frank Lightfoot's graceless comments didn't disturb her nearly so much as Manning's uncalled-for questioning of her competence. Sheri wasn't sure why she was allowing his doubts to take personal overtones. After all, Manning Chandler hadn't criticized Sheri the individual, but Sheri the professional.

Best to put her sensitivities aside and remember why she was here. The question now was whether Manning Chandler IV was going to allow her to do her job or try to make it more difficult. If he'd really given the male agents as bad a time as Frank and Anson claimed, heaven only knew what lay in store for a woman. Yet, Chandler had indicated a willingness to give her a chance. That had to count for something.

Sheri tried to focus on the book, but to no avail. She decided to give up and call Tom to provide an update on what was happening.

She finished her conversation and was returning to the lounge chair when her foot caught in the phone cord and she tripped, sending the telephone crashing to the floor.

"What the hell was that?"

Dismayed, Sheri looked up to see Manning Chandler standing in the doorway. "I'm sorry for disturbing you," she said. "I dropped the phone." Self-consciously she replaced the instrument on the desk, trying not to gawk at her client. He was wearing a navy terry-cloth bathrobe, open enough to reveal a muscular chest and short enough to display well-toned calves. His feet were bare.

He frowned, then gave a half smile. "Perhaps this is a good sign. A bodyguard who can stay awake past midnight." Manning entered the room and eased into the chair next to hers. "But, as I keep telling you people, twenty-four-hour surveillance isn't needed. I'd prefer your energies be directed toward figuring out who's behind all this nonsense."

"You hired a professional company, Mr. Chandler. This is the way we operate. Now, why don't you just take it easy and let us do what you're paying us for?"

"That's what I'd intended, but unfortunately, what with ridiculous injuries and clanging telephones—" he raised an eyebrow "—I'm spending half my time looking out for your crew instead of the other way around."

"Well, I can assure you that you won't have to watch out for me, Mr. Chandler."

"Watching you shouldn't be so difficult." His voice was low and intimate. "It's worrying about you that will tax me."

Sheri glanced over at him, about to respond, when suddenly she found herself wondering if he had anything on beneath that robe. Not much, she decided. Yet he seemed unaware of how sexy he looked at the moment, or the effect it was having on her. She'd have been a lot more comfortable if it was midday and this impromptu meeting was occurring in his office—with him fully clothed.

"You're not getting your beauty sleep." She picked up her mystery novel, hoping he'd take the hint and leave before her thoughts grew even more improper.

"Insomnia," he said. "But just because I can't sleep is no reason you shouldn't."

"I don't agree. Wallace Security believes in taking no chances. So Frank Lightfoot and I will split twelve-hour shifts." Sheri hoped her voice suggested more confidence than she actually felt in his unsettling presence. "We'll get to the bottom of these threats, Mr. Chandler. In the meantime, we'd rather you didn't interfere in our operation. I'm going to see that you're safe even if I have to spend the night in a chair by your bedroom door."

"That will hardly be necessary." His smile was teasing. "Besides, it'd be pretty difficult for a guy to

get any sleep with a beautiful woman hovering outside his bedroom.''

"I was going to offer to warm you some milk for the
insomnia," she said sweetly, "but you don't seem to
need warming up. I suggest you forget the male-female
banter. I'm immune."

"Been inoculated, huh? Bad love affair or bad
marriage?" He lifted her hand to examine her ring
finger.

Sheri jerked her hand away. "None of your business. Perhaps I'll get you that milk, after all."

"Yuck." Manning grimaced. "I think I'll just go
meekly back to my room." He started toward the
door, then paused. "By the way, don't worry about
any 'male-female' stuff. No one is more immune than
I. Tempting as you may be, I've got just about all the
women I can handle in my life. Now, I suggest you
quit playing cops and robbers and go to bed." He
turned on his heel and left.

Sheri clutched her book as she watched him go.
Well, she'd certainly set herself up for that. Forgetting her place and her position was unprofessional,
and Manning had bluntly let her know how far off
base she was. Tom and Doug could rest easy; baby
sister was in no danger from Manning Chandler. Their
wealthy client obviously preferred starlets to female
security agents.

EARLY THE NEXT MORNING Sheri bounded down the
steps in her T-shirt and shorts headed for her daily jog.
She'd just reached the front door when Manning appeared.

He gave her a restrained good-morning and a quick once-over, a look resembling disapproval on his face. He was probably subtracting more points from his already low rating of her.

Sheri was sorry she hadn't taken the time to wash her face and dab on a bit of lipstick. It was her habit simply to brush her teeth and pull her hair back in a ponytail before a workout. She'd never seen any reason to dress up to sweat—until now.

In contrast, Manning was meticulously put together, as if he was about to pose for an exercise-promotion poster. He wore a crisp spa uniform, so neat and wrinkle free it must have been freshly ironed. Not rumpled like Sheri's outfit, which had been hastily pulled from the bottom of her suitcase. To complete his perfection, his shoes—almost brand-new—matched the official navy and white of his clothes.

Belatedly it occurred to Sheri that to blend in at Fort Tranquillity, one had to wear something more spiffy than a faded T-shirt, shorts left over from high-school track and jogging shoes adorned with red Houston mud. A couple of coordinated outfits were in order if she was to look the part of a ritzy spa patron. Fortunately Fort Tranquillity had a small boutique specializing in exercise gear.

As she started out the door, Manning called to her. "Hold on a minute and I'll join you."

She looked back at him, astonished at his offer. After last night, she felt sure he'd be avoiding her. "Okay, sure. If that's what you want."

At first Sheri and Manning loped silently along at an easy pace. Slowly the exercise evolved into a test of wills, with Sheri determined to show her running companion that she could handle the strain as well as any man.

Sheri muttered a prayer of thanks for the strenuous police training she'd endured and for the fact that she'd participated in several recent marathons, including one on the Gulf Coast just a month earlier. She remembered her first race when she'd finished dead last—"dead" being the operative word. Since that early humiliation, she'd entered at least two or three a year and had even managed a decent showing in the Boston Marathon. Maybe she'd never make it to the Olympics, but her competitive spirit was alive and well.

As they continued the brisk run, Manning hardly seemed winded, and the notion that perhaps the unspoken challenge was a dumb idea began taking root in Sheri's brain. Her playboy client was obviously in great shape, which contradicted his media image of a man dedicated to carousing and late nights. There was no way he could party all the time and still remain so fit.

Sheri was beginning to wonder whether she'd overestimated her own stamina. How long did Manning intend to run, anyway? She'd lost track of how far they'd gone, but was sure they'd passed that crooked piñon tree at least three times.

They ran side by side. Chandler's breathing now almost as labored as hers. She was definitely suffering from the effects of the seven-thousand-foot altitude. "Want to stop?"

"Whenever you're ready," he countered.

"Just a little farther." She suddenly felt invigorated, as though she'd hit an exercise high, but the sensation lasted only moments. Still, she wasn't about to have Manning Chandler call her a quitter, even if this race killed her, which it soon might.

"You're not going to be able to walk tomorrow."

"Don't worry about me. I'll manage."

"Okay, let's stop."

"What?"

He halted and bent over, inhaling deeply as he spoke. "I'm not going to continue this exercise in masochism. I won't be held responsible for causing you any harm. We're quitting."

"Don't do me any favors," she gasped. She, too, was bent from the waist, trying to get more of the rarefied air into her lungs. After enduring this extended workout, was she going to be beaten at her own game? She'd only challenged him to make a point about her professionalism. "I'm tired of your accusations that our agents can't keep up with you," she told him.

"Well, not all of you can. Anson, for example, would have keeled over with a coronary by now. Don't worry, though—" he paused for breath "—it's really for my benefit that I'm stopping. You see, I can't have you dropping dead at Fort Tranquillity. It wouldn't be good for business." He gave her an engaging smile.

"Your concern is touching," she said, talking to the ground instead of him. She had to focus on his words and forget that smile. In spite of the physical punishment of the race, Sheri realized she'd actually enjoyed the competition and the time alone with Manning.

"Are you sure mouth-to-mouth resuscitation isn't needed?"

Shock at his words made Sheri lift her head. There was no mistaking the innuendo. The twinkle in his eye—and the fact that the idea seemed embarrassingly appealing—stoked her anger. "I'd sooner kiss a...a tarantula," she stammered.

Manning laughed. "I'll bet you'd scream bloody murder if you even *saw* one of those furry creatures, much less got close." He laughed again, then trotted to a nearby bench and picked up a towel, which he draped around his neck. Sauntering toward the complex, he called over his shoulder, "See you later."

As soon as he was out of sight, Sheri collapsed onto the bench, her legs still shaky from the high-altitude run and her mind fuzzy from this latest encounter with Manning. It was another five minutes before she felt revived enough to head back to the agents' quarters.

Frank greeted her when she got there. "How was the run?"

She gritted her teeth. "No comment." No need to tell Frank that his prophecy about her not being up to the demands had almost come true. Besides, there were other feelings at work here, unfamiliar, unexpected feelings that she could never share with someone like Frank. Out on the trail she'd felt close to Manning. Even when he annoyed her, she found it difficult to dislike the man. For one thing, their impromptu rivalry showed her that he had some respect for her skills. Sheri had waged too many battles for equality to fail to appreciate such treatment when it occurred.

The rest of the morning was uneventful. Frank accompanied Manning on some errands in Santa Fe, and Sheri ate breakfast in the guest dining room, then took a nap, awakening midafternoon.

"Any possibility of getting a cup of coffee?" She smiled at the cook as she stood at the doorway of the kitchen.

He glanced up from the potatoes he was peeling, but didn't bother returning the smile. "Help yourself," he said, gesturing to a large coffee urn on the counter. "Cups are in the cupboard right above you. Sugar and powdered cream, too."

"Thanks." She walked over to the coffee urn. "By the way, I'm Sheri Lindsey."

"I'm George Williams, but everyone calls me Cookie. You're new around here, aren't you?"

"Cookie?" Sheri had to stifle a grin as she thought of a character in a popular comic strip with the same nickname. The man in front of her did resemble the burly cartoon cook. Sheri forgot to answer Cookie's question until she realized he was staring at her. "I— I'm with Wallace Security."

The cook looked amused. "Ha," he snorted. "That's like sendin' a hen to watch the fox house. Since when are women bodyguards?"

"Oh, we've been around awhile." Hadn't the man ever heard of women's liberation?

"Ain't never seen a female one before."

Sheri shrugged. Apparently he hadn't. Well, that would make him fit right in with another couple of men she knew. But her job was to investigate, not to enlighten Manning Chandler's staff. She poured her coffee and wandered around, surveying the kitchen.

"Boss is in the gym," Cookie mumbled.

"Thanks, but I don't need to see him now."

"Want somethin' to eat? Lunch's over. Dinner's not till seven."

Sheri glanced at her watch. It was two-thirty. "Maybe a sandwich. I can make it, if you'll tell me where everything is."

"It's easier for me to do it myself. Tuna or ham and cheese?"

"Tuna," Sheri said. She sat on a bar stool, sipping coffee and watching. Even though Manning Chandler had run routine background checks on his employees and insisted vehemently that none of them could have sent the notes, Wallace Security had reevaluated all the staff. Both her brothers had concluded that the threats were coming from outside the facility. Sheri wasn't so certain. Something could have been overlooked. Better to suspect everyone—Cookie, for example. Was Cookie the troublemaker?

Sheri knew from their investigation that he was an ex-convict, sent to prison in his teens because of a penny-ante robbery. Unfortunately his accomplice had been armed, which elevated the crime to a felony. Once released, Cookie was without education or family. He'd drifted around for years in various short-order cooking jobs until one night Manning Chandler sampled his fare in a diner and hired him on the spot.

Chandler had given him a permanent position and was rewarded with good food and total loyalty. Sheri dismissed Cookie as a suspect. He owed Manning Chandler too much; hurting his boss would be self-defeating.

She finished the sandwich, carried the plate to the sink and raised her coffee cup. "Mind if I take this with me?"

"Help yourself," Cookie answered.

She refilled the cup and started for the door, almost colliding with a young woman. "Excuse me," Sheri said.

The newcomer glared at Sheri, who met her gaze head-on. Despite the gentle demeanor, there was animosity in the woman's eyes. The blonde, a five-foot-two-eyes-of-blue type, pulled herself up to every one of those sixty-plus inches. "Who are you?"

"Uh, Sheri Lindsey." She caught herself just in time, remembering that Manning wanted Wallace Security to keep a low profile. Since the woman wasn't wearing an employee identification badge, she must be a guest. "And you?"

"Manning didn't tell me there was a new woman here."

Sheri shrugged. "Ms . . ." she prompted.

"Angela Westin." She turned to the cook. "Cookie, I'm going to make dessert. Mr. Chandler needs cheering up, and I know lemon icebox pie's a favorite."

"We've already got pound cake."

Angela ignored him, moving past Sheri to open a cabinet drawer, taking out a white chef's apron and tying it twice around her tiny waist.

Schooled as she was in observation, Sheri couldn't help noticing Cookie's reaction to this intruder. Even though he hadn't uttered a protest, his disgruntled look said it all. Ms. Westin wasn't a bit welcome in his personal domain.

But Angela either didn't notice or didn't care. "Do you like to cook...Sheri, isn't it?"

"Sheri, it is. And no, not particularly. I'm sort of a disaster in the kitchen, so if you'll excuse me, I'll leave both of you to it."

As she made her way upstairs, Sheri wondered if Angela was Manning Chandler's girlfriend, or if she was just trying to win him over with a show of domesticity. But somehow Sheri doubted that he cared about domesticity one way or the other. She experienced a certain pleasure at the thought that Angela's culinary display would fail to impress him, then banished the idea, annoyed with herself. Why should it matter to her whether Manning Chandler cared about soufflés or saucepans? Or lemon icebox pie?

Sheri's skepticism at Angela's efforts was underscored by her lifelong disdain for the household arts. She'd seen how little the dedicated-homemaker role had helped her mother during those times when one breadwinner was gone and a replacement hadn't yet appeared. To Sheri, it seemed almost dangerous for a woman to be too domestic. No, she would have none of the "little woman" routine. Pushing the start button on the microwave and handwashing her panty hose was as close as she wanted to get.

After finishing her coffee, Sheri decided to take a leisurely tour of the house and grounds. The agents had been given guest rooms in the east wing of the administrative building, a hacienda-style house with whitewashed adobe walls and high beamed ceilings. Manning kept the west wing of the two-story structure for himself and his personal guests. The ground floor had a communal room, spacious enough for four huge couches, numerous easy chairs and a fireplace so massive Sheri could have stood up inside it. In addition, there was Manning's office, a reception area, dining room and the big country kitchen, all decorated in the distinctive colors of the Southwest—colors that reminded Sheri of a desert sunset.

She walked across a wide lawn to the fitness center. It was one of the most complete facilities she'd ever seen, containing aerobics and weight rooms, a small medical facility, an indoor track, tennis and racquetball courts, swimming pool, steam rooms, whirlpools and a sauna.

The building was flanked by a cluster of cabanas and a large dormitory in the same adobe as the rest of the complex. The dorm had apartments for permanent staff and suites for paying guests, plus the boutique and the immense dining room where she'd had breakfast. Outside, in another pool, a spa employee was conducting a water-aerobics class for a group of senior citizens. Beside the pool were more tennis and racquetball courts and, off to the left, she saw a stable that housed the Fort's horses. A pretty pinto munched grass in the adjoining corral. Circling the whole complex and winding up into the mountains was the path on which Sheri had challenged her host that morning.

With a cooler head—and muscles that were beginning to protest—Sheri realized the trail was better
suited for walking or hiking than running. Manning
Chandler could have warned her about it, instead of
allowing her to make a fool of herself. *That's not fair,
Sheri. You shouldn't blame your lack of judgment on
the client.*

She tried to force her mind off the man in question
and onto the magnificent view of the rolling foothills
dotted with piñon and aspen, and a sky as blue as a
perfectly dyed Easter egg. The effort succeeded only
fleetingly before her thoughts were back on Manning
Chandler. Sheri couldn't help thinking how nice it
must be to have wealthy parents subsidizing you, since
few people had the means to start a project as large as
this one. Even Wallace Security, with its unpreten-
tious beginning, couldn't have gotten under way
without a long-term bank loan.

After her tour was complete, Sheri spent the rest of
her day studying pictures of the staff, so she could
identify them, and reading their résumés, so she'd
know something about each one. She had to admit
Manning had taken careful security measures. Not
only were employees required to wear name tags, but
his initial background checks on them, done as a condition of employment, were thorough. According to
Frank, their client had said he wouldn't risk the privacy or well-being of his high-profile guests by hiring
haphazardly.

The whole group—Manning, his assistant Juan,
Sheri, Frank and a couple of guests, including Angela—ate together in the headquarters' dining room

that evening. Dinner was a nicely turned out prime rib with potatoes, steamed carrots and green peas, a tossed salad and whole-wheat rolls. And for dessert, Angela's lemon pie and Cookie's pound cake.

It was a perfect opportunity for Sheri to size up everyone under the guise of getting better acquainted. A few discreet questions in a social setting would attract little attention. Sheri couldn't help speculating about the relationship between Manning and Angela. Certainly friendly, yet somehow Sheri didn't sense that it was serious—at least not for him. He didn't act like a man in love. Still, he was charming and considerate to the woman.

Come to think of it, he was charming and considerate to everyone tonight. Sheri felt disconcerted. Before arriving in New Mexico, she'd been sure she had a fix on Manning—a rich man's son, spoiled, indulged, used to being catered to. The description no longer seemed appropriate. There was definitely more than one side to his nature.

As Sheri reflected on this other Manning, she had to admit he was popular with his staff, even the caustic Cookie.

She glanced around the table, mentally reviewing what she had gleaned about each of the guests from her predecessors' reports. Everyone present had been dismissed as a potential suspect. After personal contact with them, Sheri agreed with the other agency's observations. There seemed to be no threat here. The only person she wasn't sure of was Angela. Yet the feeling was closer to jealousy than any other emotion

Sheri could identify. She couldn't seem to react rationally to the woman.

Dinner was relaxed. Manning's stories about his experiences at a boys' prep school in Houston got the conversation going, and it went on for an hour after the meal was cleared. Then the diners began trailing away, Sheri bound for the study, Frank wandering out to the staff quarters for a poker game with Cookie and some of the trainers. Angela drove into Santa Fe with Juan, pouting because Manning refused to come. He didn't join the cardplayers, either; to Sheri's surprise, he retreated to his suite.

Sheri settled down with her novel, the television set humming softly in the corner, but she had difficulty concentrating. Her stiffening muscles continued to ache from the morning workout and her thoughts could neither escape nor solve the puzzle of Manning Chandler.

Just when she'd decided she had him figured out, he fooled her. If the past two days were any indication, he definitely wasn't the party goer portrayed in the society pages. Quite the opposite, he seemed to practice an early-to-bed, early-to-rise philosophy. And, as far as she could tell, he spent those hours in bed alone. Not only was Manning friendly with staff and guests, for the most part, he treated her and Frank the same way. All in all he didn't act the part of the high-and-mighty pampered playboy she'd expected.

It was disconcerting not to be able to effectively gauge him, as if her usual analytical and observational skills had abandoned her. Could her brothers' comments about this client have affected her judgment? Or was Manning's attractiveness starting to short-circuit her thought processes? Whichever, she felt confused. Sheri was accustomed to being in control—of her emotions and of the situation. It bothered her that she was so dramatically uncertain when it came to Chandler.

She stood up, twisting her body and arching her back as she tried to work out a few kinks. Then she sank into the armchair again and pondered the assignment. Manning had gone to the trouble of hiring two different security companies, yet behaved as though he was in absolutely no danger, mingling confidently with his patrons and making junkets around the countryside without any consideration for safety. One would think he'd display a bit more concern about the threats. Was he foolhardy? Or didn't he take them seriously?

On cue, as if her thoughts had conjured him up out of thin air, Manning appeared and flopped down in the chair beside her. "Lonesome?"

"Not really," she said, glancing up briefly, then returning her eyes to the book. "More insomnia?" Although it was early, Manning was again in his bathrobe.

"No, I just thought I'd keep you company." He plucked the book from her hand and folded a corner of the page before laying it on the table. "You don't play poker?"

"Occasionally, but I prefer reading. And I'm still on duty."

"I figured as much. But why here? Did you decide against camping outside my room?"

"No, I'm doing my best to adhere to your instructions. I'm trying to ensure that you're not burdened by too much protection."

He pursed his lips in amusement. "I think I could get used to having a little protection," he finally said. "From someone like you, that is. Those guys you work with aren't exactly my type." He smiled, a damnably appealing smile.

Sheri had folded her legs under her, causing her green skirt to inch up, baring her knees. Now she placed her feet on the floor and straightened in the chair. "My job isn't a joke, you know." Her voice was indignant.

"Sorry," he apologized, somewhat unconvincingly, as his eyes wandered around the room. "Is this how you spend most of your nights?" Before she could say anything, he added, "Doesn't the quiet bother you?"

She looked at him. "No, I don't mind the quiet. In fact, I rather like it."

"But you don't like me, do you?"

She eyed him warily. "I really hadn't given it much thought."

"Right," he agreed sarcastically. "You just give the cold shoulder to all your clients."

"Mr. Chandler. I am not here as your companion or to provide entertainment when one of your girlfriends isn't around. Whether I like you or not is irrelevant. I'm here to find out who's sending those letters and, if necessary, to protect you." Sheri gave herself a mental pat on the back. She was a profes-

sional and she'd make sure Manning Chandler understood that.

"That was a priggish little speech," he said. "Why
do I have the feeling you might not mind so much if
something did happen to me?"

"Believe me, I'd mind. To quote someone I heard
recently, 'It wouldn't be good for business.'"

Manning threw back his head and laughed heartily.
"At last an honest response. Touché, Ms. Lindsey."
He rose from his chair. "Need anything from downstairs? I'm hungry. Thought I'd raid the refrigerator."

"Maybe some fruit or yogurt. I'll go with you. I
need to stretch my legs."

His brow furrowed. "Stretch your legs or keep an
eye on me?"

"You sure are suspicious, aren't you?"

"I've told you it's not necessary to dog my every
step."

"And I've agreed with you. But even if I *was* doing
that, what would be the harm?"

He scowled more deeply, "I thought you said you
weren't going to overdo it. I plan to turn on all the
lights, and I won't wander around in the dark where
some big bad bogeyman might get me. But if it'll make
you feel better, come along."

She followed him down the stairs. "Why aren't you
taking these threats seriously?"

"Oh, but I am. Why else would I hire you?"

"Why indeed? I've been asking myself the same
question, especially since you seem intent on hinder-

ing our ability to do the job. We need to question your guests—"

"No way," he cut in. "Just focus on the fact that there's probably less danger to me personally than to my business if word of a security problem gets out." He opened the freezer and pulled out a carton of frozen strawberry yogurt, then moved to the cabinet to take down a couple of bowls.

"A lot of the people who come here are famous. If they had any idea there was cause for alarm, it could be devastating, possibly even result in the spa folding, heaven forbid. The thought of returning to the corporate world frightens me more than some crackpot does." He handed Sheri a bowl of yogurt, then replaced the carton in the freezer.

They sat at the counter, silently eating. Sheri wished she weren't so aware of him. He was definitely getting under her skin, and try as she might, Manning Chandler was impossible to ignore.

THE HIGH-ALTITUDE RUN continued to cause Sheri's muscles to ache throughout the next day, her legs rebelling with every step. The minute she was off duty, she slipped on a swimsuit and robe, then limped over to the fitness center to take advantage of the whirlpool.

She'd brought her novel along and was leaning against the side of the pool, her legs floating in front of her. She'd only read a few pages when Manning's voice sounded behind her. "Therapy time?"

Sheri gave him a quick glance. He was wearing a red swimsuit and his muscular chest was bare. He eased into the pool, moving through the water until he was next to her.

"Can I tear you away from your book for a moment?"

Sheri closed the book and tossed it over to a dry area. "Something on your mind?"

He sat back like Sheri, his legs floating free. "As a matter of fact, this seems the perfect time to talk about the qualifications of your crew." He turned toward her. "Or maybe I should simply mention the latest arrival, the lady who goes around offering challenges and pulling stupid stunts.... By the way, are you all right? Any leg pain?"

His knowing question brought Sheri up short, but she had to concede he was definitely on target. "I'll live. I'll even own up to the fact that I should have had more sense. But me aside, what about the qualifications of the Wallace agents?"

"The incident with you has just confirmed my opinion that your people aren't tough enough to handle everything that goes with the job. There have been mishaps with almost all of you."

Sheri straightened and looked at him. "I'm glad you mentioned that. Can you explain why we don't have any of these problems on our other assignments? Could it be that *you're* contributing to the accidents? You, after all, have more experience with the altitude and terrain."

"And how does that make me responsible? Take you, for example. How am I to blame for *that* attack of lunacy?"

"Yes, I made a mistake chasing you around the mountain, but then again, perhaps you should've stopped things sooner."

"Oh, no, you're not hanging that on me. If I've done anything wrong, it was hiring Wallace in the first place. After the problems with the other group, I should have known better. Just because you guard touring rock musicians or occupy the security desk at one of my father's businesses doesn't mean you're equipped for the kind of life I lead. You're not trained for it." He finished his statement with a shrug.

"What do you mean 'not trained'? That's ridiculous. My own education has been extensive—a degree in sociology, then the police academy, seminars, not to mention years of on-the-job training. As for the others, both Frank and Pete were military police, and Anson was a Houston police officer."

"Before he retired."

Sheri nodded.

"You didn't hear me. Before he retired. Anson needs a desk job. I don't want to belittle him. He was undoubtedly a hell of a cop, but even if I were in real danger—and for the record, I don't believe I am— Anson's too out of shape to handle it. As for your former military police, their experience probably consisted of standing watch at the gate of some base or escorting drunken servicemen out of bars. Not one of you is up to the rigors of Fort Tranquillity."

"Sure," Sheri said. "Blame all the misfortune on everyone else. Let yourself off the hook." She felt obligated to defend her staff, but privately she had to admit there might be some truth to his accusations.

"I'm not trying to assign blame. I just want everything back to normal. After years of doing what others expected, I'm finally leading my own life. Or I was, until I started getting a series of crazy notes warning me that someone's planning to do me in.

"So, I hire Wallace to help me avoid trouble and I end up with a bunch of walking disasters, who do nothing for my peace of mind and get themselves hurt chasing phantoms or showing off. Take the pretty-boy agent who got into that patch of poison ivy. If he'd stuck to the trail like I instructed, instead of beating the bushes looking for bad guys, he'd have been okay. And Garcia's dislocated shoulder, well, he was trying to impress one of the guests and got overzealous with the weights. In the meantime, nobody has a clue about the letter-writing wacko. Then you come along, acting like some sort of Jane Wayne."

Sheri was surprised he was familiar with that term; few people outside law-enforcement circles were. Psychologists had coined the phrase "John Wayne syndrome" to describe officers who never took off their badges, those who talked, thought and breathed police work, twenty-four hours a day, seven days a week.

"Jane Wayne" was the female counterpart, but Sheri didn't apply the expression to herself. She actually had many other interests, but unfortunately Manning was only seeing her in a single role and generalizing from it. He seemed determined to paint her and the Wallace team in a bad light, but she was just as determined to stand up for herself and her colleagues.

"And I suppose the broken leg was the agent's fault, too? Did you ever consider altering your activities a bit to accommodate us?"

Manning raised his hands in frustration. "What's the use of trying to explain anything to you?" He moved closer, until he was almost nose to nose with her. "Listen, *Agent* Lindsey. I've spent years building the kind of life I want. A life different from what I grew up with, a life I like much better. Here, I'm surrounded by a group of people who care about me— for me. I don't want it spoiled—not by some cowardly kook, and not by incompetent investigators who want me to change my existence in order to simplify theirs. I'm not asking you to do anything but your job. If you can," he added for good measure, before grabbing a towel and leaving the whirlpool.

Sheri sat there stunned as he stormed off. She felt more bruised than ever. Perhaps her muscles had benefited from the soaking, but her psyche was definitely damaged by his reprimand. Sighing, she pulled herself out of the water, noticing her legs and feet with dismay. "You stayed in so long, you look like a prune," she muttered to herself as she tugged on her robe and hurried to her suite.

CHAPTER THREE

THE NEXT MORNING, Sheri walked to Manning's office, her stance rigid, her expression stern. After their confrontation at the whirlpool, he appeared to be avoiding her, spending most of the previous day in town talking with potential clients. He'd returned to the Fort just to change clothes before going back to Santa Fe with several of the guests, including Angela. He might have decided he could put Sheri out of the picture, but the only way he was going to accomplish that was to sever all connections with Wallace Security.

He glanced up as she entered. "Legs feeling better?"

"I feel fine," Sheri said. "Despite your doubts, I happen to be in good physical condition and all the aches and pains have gone away. Was concern for my health the reason you failed to advise me of your scheduled expedition into the wilderness today?"

Manning looked momentarily nonplussed. "I'm trying to cooperate. At my request, Frank's coming along to baby-sit."

"Since when are you in charge of our job assignments? How would you like it if I started ordering your staff around?"

"Point well-taken," he said. "So, come yourself if you prefer. Whatever. I'm leaving within the hour."

Sheri stared at him. Now what? Her common sense said to back down, to let Frank go. But common sense seemed to take a holiday in her dealings with Manning Chandler. "Where are you headed?"

"I need to scout around for a rappelling site closer to the Fort."

"Why?"

"Because I usually have to take people into Colorado, and a closer one would be more convenient. Well, if you're coming with me, you'd better get moving. We'll be gone overnight."

"Who's 'we'?"

"Just you and me."

"But..."

"What's the problem, Ms. Lindsey? Afraid of being alone in the woods with me?"

"That's not it at all," Sheri denied, although the idea *was* rather frightening. "But it makes no sense for the two of us to go off like that when someone's sending you ominous warnings."

"I can't hide inside the Fort for the rest of my life. Now be a good girl and hurry it up. Oh, and tell Cookie to put together a couple of meals." He waved Sheri out of the office and began making a call.

After throwing a few belongings into a bag and advising Frank she'd be replacing him on the trip, Sheri waited in the kitchen for Cookie to finish packing their meals for the trail. At this instant, she couldn't help but rue the day she'd come to New Mexico. It seemed that she'd lost complete control of the situation. She didn't want to go camping, and she especially didn't want to go camping with Manning. In the first place, she thought it was foolhardy, and secondly, she had no desire to isolate herself with him.

Heaven only knew how he'd behave when they were completely alone. Heaven only knew how *she'd* behave. Even though she didn't want to get involved with any man right now, and even though this particular man was totally exasperating, Sheri realized how attracted she was to Manning Chandler. She couldn't deny it any longer. She wanted his respect, his admiration for her work and...what else? She suddenly felt flustered, confused.

Just how impressed is he going to be, she admonished herself, *once he finds out that your one and only camping experience was a Girl Scout retreat when you were twelve?* It looked as though she'd have to bluff her way through this trip. With a little luck, her secret would remain safe, and Chandler would be denied another reason to complain about the incompetence of Wallace Security agents.

She suspected him of manufacturing this spur-of-the-moment outing simply to make a Wallace Security agent miserable, but she'd be darned if she'd let him know how successful his efforts were. She was already miserable, and they hadn't even left the Fort. And the worst was yet to come, of that she was certain. A city girl, Sheri knew virtually nothing about camping, only enough to realize that anyplace without electricity and indoor plumbing was not for her. Until now she'd successfully avoided such places, since all of the Wallace's previous clients had been as committed to modern amenities as she.

When Manning met her at the back gate with a monstrous black stallion and a slightly smaller palomino, she knew he expected her to panic and bolt. He was probably attempting to teach her a thing or two about inviting herself on other people's trips. Well, she would give him no satisfaction at this juncture. Instead, she calmly handed him one of the rolled sleeping bags stacked on the porch, fastened the other to the back of her saddle, then swung herself up. It was fortunate Manning couldn't see her face and the smug smile she wore. At least once, she'd managed to surprise him.

She could ride because she'd taken lessons, first when she was going through an adolescent love affair with horses, and then a refresher course in college, thinking she might join a mounted police unit. Many large cities fielded corps of officers on horseback, and she had wanted to cover that option.

They rode for more than two hours, finally stopping at a clearing near the top of a small waterfall. Sheri wished she'd brought her camera to capture the rough beauty of the northern New Mexico countryside. But learning about the trip at the last minute had barely given her time to grab a toothbrush and underwear.

As they dismounted, she rubbed her backside, relieved that the ride had ended. Her seat was becoming numb, and her legs, still sore from the jogging of two days ago—despite her little white lie to the contrary—now protested after being in the same position for so long.

The higher elevation was cool enough to require a camp fire, and while Manning collected firewood, Sheri strolled around, enjoying the view of jagged pines and pockmarked cliffs.

"Don't tire yourself out making camp," Manning said sarcastically.

She sent him a withering look and continued to enjoy her surroundings. What was there to do, anyway? Correction, what was there to do that she *could* do? Her Girl Scout training wasn't much help, since the only memory she retained was that of browning marshmallows on the end of a stick. She could just imagine Manning's reaction if she mentioned marshmallow roasting as the high mark in her wilderness experience.

Suddenly her foot connected with something soft and definitely snakelike, and she let out a piercing scream.

"Good Lord!" Manning came racing over. "What's wrong?"

"A snake!"

"Where?"

"Right there." Sheri pointed to the place where her foot just rested. "It's gone." Her heart was still beating furiously.

"The poor thing," Manning said. "You probably scared it to death. I'm surprised a little ol' varmint upset you," he added with a grin, "considering your penchant for tarantula kissing."

Sheri groaned silently. Not only was the man obnoxious, but he apparently remembered everything she said. "You're all heart."

"Well, more than likely it was harmless, if it *was* a snake. Just don't bother it, and it won't bother you." He started toward the fire pit, then turned back. "How about a walk before I light the fire?"

She shrugged noncommittally. "You're the boss." Sheri wasn't keen on traipsing through the woods, but she *was* supposed to be the bodyguard. Besides, it didn't appear that lounging around camp would be any safer, not when it put her almost at eye level with things that slithered.

They walked for about a mile, and Manning showed her some of the flora and fauna native to the area. Despite herself, Sheri enjoyed their trek—when she wasn't watching for snakes. She knew it would be imprudent to ask if there might be any more reptilian types here in the woods, mainly because she didn't want to know the answer.

It finally occurred to her that she was neglecting her duty, failing to remain on the alert for potential harm to her client. She recalled Manning's statement that he spent most of his time watching out for the security agents, instead of the other way around. In this one instance his criticism was accurate, and the realization stung.

The sun was just setting when they returned to the campsite. Sheri had overcome her fear of wriggly creatures enough to sit on her still-rolled sleeping bag and watch the changing patterns of pink and orange as the sun disappeared beneath the horizon. As dusk deepened into darkness, Manning lighted the fire and they sat in front of it, eating turkey sandwiches and drinking hot coffee from a thermos.

Except for the occasional ominous sound coming from the woods and the pesky insects, it was a serene environment. However, even discounting the sounds and the insects, she and Manning were not a relaxed pair. There was an underlying current between them, a constant tension that was far more personal than professional.

Manning finally spoke. "I'm glad you invited yourself along. You're probably a better camping buddy than Lightfoot. I'd be willing to bet he's worthless in the wild." He paused before adding, "Unlike you."

"I was beginning to think you were going to say something nice about Wallace Security, but as usual you managed to come through with another barb."

"Just a little joke, Agent Lindsey. I'm actually pleased that we have a chance to talk privately, without any concern that someone can overhear." He broke a twig off a nearby bush and nervously twirled it in his fingers, his expression becoming pained before he flung the twig aside. "It kills me to say this, but I'm beginning to suspect the threats are coming from inside. Damn..." He picked up a pebble and tossed it in the direction of the waterfall, as if he needed something to keep his hands occupied. "Maybe I'm paranoid, but I've even started wondering whether my phone's tapped or my office is bugged."

"You mean you think someone on your staff is sending those notes?"

He nodded. "I'm almost certain of it, and the notion is driving me crazy. I feel close to every last one of them. It's like having a family member turn against you." He paused. "No, with my family, that's not a good analogy. It's like having a good friend turn against you."

That was the second time he'd alluded to a less-than-perfect family situation. But she didn't feel she knew him well enough to probe for details. "So, what made you change your mind? You were so positive it was an outsider."

"I know. I suppose I was adamant because that's what I wanted to believe. But it's become obvious the letters were generated here. I got another one a couple of mornings ago."

Sheri began to comment, but was hushed by Manning.

"Don't say it. I realize I should have given it to you, but I wanted to check something first. I'm positive this one was typed on an old typewriter we keep in the fitness office. It doesn't close the letter *e*."

Sheri toyed with her sandwich wrapper, then rolled it into a ball and put it into a makeshift garbage bag. "What kind of ribbon does the typewriter have? If it's a onetime carbon, we can take it off and analyze it. Maybe even pinpoint when the letter was written. You didn't happen to bring it, did you?"

Manning grinned. "You get caught up in all this, don't you?"

"It *is* my job. And you've wasted valuable time. You've got to understand how important it is to turn over evidence immediately."

"Hold on. I'm as anxious to catch the traitor as you are, you know."

The tone of Manning's voice, his restless energy and his use of the word "traitor" revealed emotions in him that she wasn't sure how to handle. She decided it would be best to focus on Wallace's role. "Do Tom and Doug know?"

"No, I've told no one but you."

Sheri wondered if the knowledge about the typewriter had contributed to his ill humor the morning at the sauna. "At least we have something to go on now. I'll talk to Frank as soon as we get back, and we'll intensify our surveillance." She and Manning discussed the situation for another half hour or so, then she stood up and stretched. "I think I'll turn in."

Manning also stood. "That's a good idea. We have a full day tomorrow." He shoved his hands into the pockets of his jeans and gazed into the darkness. "I didn't see anything acceptable for rappelling this afternoon, but we'll keep looking. Have you ever tried it?"

Sheri shook her head. Manning seemed to be putting off saying good-night, as if he was enjoying her company and didn't want the evening to end.

There was a long, embarrassed silence as they stared into one another's eyes. Then, slowly, the tension she'd felt changed into something else. An excited anticipation... They moved closer together, until Manning finally reached out and pulled her toward him.

His hands slid over her rib cage until one hand connected with the shoulder holster under her jacket. "That's a gun!" he shouted, breaking the embrace like someone who'd touched a hot stove.

Sheri was startled by his rejection and paused before answering, "Of course it's a gun."

"Well, get rid of it. I don't like them."

"That's too bad," she said, "because I need it for my job. I'm not wearing a thirty-eight as a fashion accessory, you know."

"You're not going to wear it at all! I can't afford a shoot-out in front of my guests."

"Do you see any guests around right now? Besides, whoever's sending you those menacing letters may be dangerous."

"I doubt that," he said stubbornly. "If it is someone on staff, then I'm sure I'm in no danger. Whoever's making threats is misguided, but not a risk. I'd bet on that."

"You might be betting your life. A few days ago you were certain the culprit *wasn't* an employee. I don't want to take any chances."

"That's where we differ, because I'm willing to take the chance. And since *I* hired *you,* not vice versa, you'd better go along with my wishes. Get rid of the gun," he ordered again. When Sheri glared at him obstinately, he relented, "At least while you're inside the Fort."

Later that night, Sheri lay in her sleeping bag, barely four feet away from Manning, struggling to regain her perspective and trying to assess why this assignment was anything but a textbook case. One reason was her strong empathy for Manning. Seeing his pain hurt her, made her angry that one of his workers would victim- ize him. Who could it be? Someone close? Someone like Juan? Surely not. Juan appeared to be his most trusted confidant. And she'd already ruled out Cookie. True, the man had a record, but his affection for his boss was obvious.

It had to be someone else. Unfortunately the list of possibilities was long—the Fort was a large operation with dozens of employees. And on the surface, any- way, they'd all checked out. Fascinating as the puzzle was, it was becoming more and more difficult for Sheri to separate the job from the man.

No matter how she tried to squelch it, her attrac- tion to Manning kept coming to the forefront. Their near kiss had simply stoked a growing fire that flared up whenever he was around. There was an awareness, a sexual intensity, unlike any Sheri had experienced in other relationships. She'd dated a number of interest- ing men, but there had never been any real chemistry, and she hadn't fantasized about a male since high school, when the sophomore class president replaced horses as the object of her attentions. So, what was there about Manning? Why did she find herself thinking of her client in altogether inappropriate ways?

Gazing up at the stars arrayed like Christmas lights in the dark expanse of sky, Sheri analyzed these new and unfamiliar feelings. She realized how limited her life had become lately. Counting on her fingers, she calculated how long it had been since her last date. Months. At least four months. But with her work schedule and other activities, it was difficult to have much of a social life.

Not that there weren't opportunities every now and then. Glen Henderson, one of the new agents in Houston, had made his attraction clear on more than one occasion, but Sheri didn't plan on dating Glen or any of the agents. It would create too many problems. She'd always have to wonder whether the men were attracted to her for herself or because of her position in the company.

And then there were the complications created by her work. Agents were often together on assignments, spending days or nights—albeit fully dressed and on duty—alone. Friendship was all that she would permit. Romantic relationships would just confuse matters, perhaps even compromise an assignment.

For those reasons, it had been one of Sheri's decisions to steer clear of personal entanglements with Wallace employees. A decision she had no intention of changing.

Unfortunately she had few opportunities to get to know men off the job. When not working, she jogged, attended movies with girlfriends, visited her family, taught a crime-prevention class and volunteered in a local girls' organization. Few eligible men came into the picture.

Not that she didn't have Tom and Doug trying their hands at matchmaking. Meddling in her life was a given for them. Friends tried, too. Her best friend, Helen, had been pushing a cousin for months. But Sheri wasn't interested. And if she had been? Well, her career would probably serve as a deterrent, anyway. It often did.

The typical response to a question about her occupation was "You're kidding," followed by a joke about whether she was another "V. I. Warshawski," then more questions about whom she protected or the weapons she used and where she carried them. Her answers usually provided entertainment and satisfied people's curiosity, but when it came to pursuing a relationship, men seemed put off by her protector role and suspicious of her long hours with other males.

So, Sheri concluded, after a very unromantic four months, it was natural for her to be attracted to someone as handsome as Manning Chandler. Even if she didn't need a man in her life right now, it didn't mean she would never need a man—a husband, children. She just didn't want to make the same mistakes her mother had. She wanted *one* husband for fifty years or so, not a series of them with short-term contracts. She pushed thoughts of her mother aside; after all, it was getting late and tomorrow would be a busy day.

Sheri awakened before dawn. Manning was already up, settled on a boulder, drinking coffee and gazing at the sunrise. Sheri sat up in her sleeping bag so she could watch, too. The chance to enjoy nature in this quiet leisurely way was a fringe benefit of camping she'd never considered before.

After a breakfast of peanut butter on English muffins, washed down with several cups of coffee, Sheri and Manning packed their gear and began the search for the rappelling site. They rode in tandem, Sheri's horse following Manning's along the narrow trail as he scouted the area for suitable cliffs. There was no conversation, merely an occasional gesture to indicate a direction or a stop.

Manning seemed to be in a world of his own, and Sheri could only guess what he was thinking about. This was a man lost in his love for the wilderness and its serenity. Sheri envied his ability to put other concerns aside and appreciate his surroundings. She doubted she would be so calm and relaxed if she was the one confronted with a traitor.

She began to review the information she had on the Fort's staff. But this wasn't really the place to do that. She needed the file in front of her, needed to study the minute details, which could provide a clue. She might as well content herself with savoring the ride and reflecting on the beauty of the countryside.

Sheri hadn't fared too badly at camping, if she did say so herself. Except for overreacting to the snake, she'd held her own out here. A real accomplishment for a city girl. She'd expected to suffer stoically through the trip, and to actually enjoy most of it was serendipitous. She knew Manning's company was part of the reason. She couldn't forget their almost kiss. It had left her with a longing, an unfilled need. Sheri gave her head a quick shake. It was better not to think about that.

They'd ridden for most of the morning, checking out several possible rappelling sites. None satisfied Manning, but he didn't seem disappointed on the ride back to the Fort. "I'll keep looking. There's plenty of time, since we've got the place in Colorado to fall back on." He smiled at the pun.

Now Sheri could see the Fort in the distance. She'd learned a lot about Manning Chandler over the past twenty-four hours, a lot about the investigation—and a lot about herself.

"Thanks for the company." Manning dismounted and handed the reins to one of the stable boys, then helped Sheri down from her horse. "I'll get that letter for you right away."

"Good," Sheri said. The trip seemed to have created a relationship of respect between Manning and her, and as a result he appeared to have regained some confidence in Wallace Security.

JUST WHEN SHERI was basking in the newfound regard that Manning Chandler had for Wallace Security, another accident occurred. The day after their return, Manning's morning activity had been a ten-mile mountain hike with a group of guests.

The casualty this time was Frank Lightfoot, who'd taken it on himself to check out the route before the hike began and was, therefore, dog tired when the actual trek started. Winded, his concentration diminished, Frank slipped on loose rocks, which sprained his foot and caused ligament damage and meant he had to hobble all the way back to the Fort. His foot was doubling in size and discoloring fiercely when Manning helped him into a kitchen chair, removed his boot and sock while Sheri filled an ice pack. At the fridge she berated herself for doing paperwork, instead of going along.

"Lightfoot," Manning quipped, "this swollen hoof of yours looks like it weighs ten pounds. You may have to get a name change."

Frank grimaced. "That's exactly what I need, humor in the face of my pain and suffering."

"Didn't mean to add to your distress," Manning said with a trace of contrition. "You are a little peaked." He himself seemed none the worse for wear, his clothes and appearance as fresh as if he'd simply been out for a morning stroll. But his set expression indicated that he wasn't pleased with this latest course of events.

"I can't believe a firm with the reputation of Wallace's would send out such a bunch of bumblers," he muttered to Sheri as he passed the refrigerator to retrieve a kitchen stool. "I don't know why you people can't keep up."

"It was an accident," Sheri said, feeling defensive. "And I believe I've kept up with you pretty well—except for a bit of overambitious jogging."

"Where I was forced to put a stop to your foolishness. I must admit I was surprised you didn't fall off the horse when we were camping." Manning sent a stony glare her way, then returned to Frank, carefully lifting his heel to rest on the stool. "Sorry, old buddy, but I think you'll be off your feet for a while. I'll have the clinic send over some crutches. In the meantime, you have no choice but to take it easy."

"Great," Frank said bitterly. "I can just imagine what Anson's going to say about another replacement."

"No more replacements," Manning shot back. "This is it."

"That's impossible," Sheri protested as she brought over the ice pack. "Your contract—"

"I'm beginning to regret signing that damn contract." He glowered at both of them. "It seemed so reasonable, so simple—find out the identity of that demented pen pal of mine. Instead, the guy's probably laughing himself silly. I should probably rechristen the place Fort Calamity."

Sheri cringed, silently admitting that he had a point. Wallace was messing up royally, but why? They'd never had a problem like this before. Manning wasn't the only one who was regretting the agreement. She wished she could turn tail and head back for the dependable routine of Houston. For now, though, she needed to salvage the assignment as best she could. "There won't be any more accidents," she assured him with bravado. "And we *will* get to the bottom of those threats."

"Seems I've heard that song before."

"One more chance?" Sheri's voice was soft, pleading. She just couldn't go back to Texas and admit to her brothers she'd failed.

"One more," Manning relented, "but forget about replacements. Lightfoot can stay around and lick his wounds while you trail after me. But that's it. Do I make myself clear?"

"Perfectly," she said, relieved and resigned.

SHERI WAS CONDUCTING an interior inspection when she spotted a stranger heading toward Manning's of-

fice. The man was six feet tall and muscular, with un-
kempt hair and a scraggly beard. He was dressed in
dusty well-worn jeans and mud-caked boots. Danger
was written all over him.

How had the man slipped through security? She
approached him cautiously, managing to block his
way. "Can I help you?"

The man eyed her suggestively. "Not now, honey.
Where's Chandler?"

"May I ask the nature of your business?" Sheri's
hand surreptitiously eased toward her revolver. The
revolver she was glad she still carried, despite Manning's order.

"That, little lady, is none of your concern." He
took her by the shoulders to move her aside.

In an instant, Sheri had the man's arm twisted behind him and his face pressed against the wall. "Security. Identify yourself. *Now!*"

"You've got to be kidding. Chandler," he yelled
out, "are you in there? Call off the watchdog!"

Manning flung open the door of his office. Blue
eyes shocked, he surveyed the scene. "What the *hell*
are you doing?" he demanded.

She loosened her hold. "I, uh . . ."

"Back off," Manning ordered, pulling her away.

The stranger stretched out his arm and carefully
rotated his shoulder, then flashed an insolent grin at
Sheri. "I guess nothing's broken, tiger, but I'm used
to women handling me a bit more delicately." He
leered again at Sheri before turning to Manning.
"Aren't you going to introduce us, Chandler?"

"This is Race Evans," Manning said to Sheri.

Sheri almost groaned when she heard the name. He was only the most popular soap-opera star in the country.

"Race doesn't usually look like this," Manning explained. "The beard and long hair are for his new film. Race, meet Sheri Lindsey."

Now she remembered reading in a gossip column that the television idol was making the transition to movies. He'd obviously been filming a Western nearby.

"Pleased to meet you—I think." He rubbed his shoulder gingerly. "Is she really security, Manning? She sure doesn't look like a cop."

"Well, you ought to be the first to agree she acts like one," Manning countered. "Why don't you go on over to the fitness center and use the whirlpool, Race? I'll be there in a minute. I need to see Ms. Lindsey first."

Sheri was subdued. Clearly she'd made a mistake, but the guy could have doubled as a frontier-style mercenary, and it was her job to protect Manning. Still, an apology appeared to be in order. "Sorry," she said to Manning as Race left.

He put up his hand to silence her. " 'Sorry' doesn't cut it." Manning's expression was grim. "Race Evans and his crowd are my best clients. Another mistake like that and I won't have to worry about business, because there won't *be* any business."

"I said I was sorry," Sheri answered through clenched teeth.

He shook his head. "And I say that won't do. I told you and your Keystone Kops pals that I'm not satisfied with your work, and this fiasco is the final straw. When you start attacking my clients, it's clear you've outlived your usefulness. So, I suggest you start packing. Contract or no contract, I intend to clean house today."

He paused to glare at her. "After your stupid stunt with Race," he went on, "I'll probably be the laughingstock of the industry. I've decided that I don't need an investigator. I especially don't need an investigator who's suspicious of everyone in pants." With that Manning stomped out.

Sheri was speechless, her mind unsettled by his angry comments. Manning Chandler was definitely overreacting. Then her confusion changed to distress as she realized that the attack was personal, painfully so. She wanted nothing more than to do what he suggested—pack up and leave. Like every professional, she'd had to deal with complaints now and then, but this client's criticism, and even worse, his disappointment, hurt more. Why? *Shake it off,* she told herself. *This is business. Don't let your feelings interfere with your job. Give the man some time to cool down.*

Even more important, she had to figure out a way to get him to rescind his marching orders. That was easier said than done. He'd been furious enough to throttle her; to convince him he was being unreasonable would take real diplomacy.

Several hours had passed when the intercom buzzed and Manning summoned her to his office. Sheri pulled out her compact, then paused. "What am I doing?" She shoved the case into her purse, rose from her chair and strode to his office, back straight, chin up, ready to face more of Chandler's abuse. She'd give the man an opportunity to vent his anger, but she wasn't about to grovel. The entire Wallace Security contingent would be out of here by sunset if that was what he *really* wanted.

Manning was filling out some kind of report when she arrived and knocked on the door frame. He glanced up. "Come in."

Sheri walked over to his desk, standing until he motioned her to sit down.

"I've been thinking about what happened this morning. And I'm reconsidering my position." He paused, tapping his pen on the desk. "Maybe I was too harsh. Race seems to think the whole thing was pretty funny. After I explained the situation here, he reminded me that you were only doing your job." Manning looked directly at her, his expression thoughtful. "I admit I get a little upset when I feel my business is at risk. Actually you haven't done that badly. Plus, we've been getting along well—most of the time, anyway. Race promised to keep your reasons for being here under his hat. So, what do you say we just put the episode behind us. Okay?"

Sheri was shocked. She'd come to his office expecting another reprimand and wondering how she was going to handle the situation, yet here he was being almost conciliatory. "Okay," she answered, trying to prevent a relieved smile from spreading across her face.

They stared at each other for long uncomfortable seconds before she finally said, "Well, if that's all, I'll get back to work."

"That's all."

Sheri returned to her desk in the detail office. Despite the reprieve and her temporary elation, she kept remembering the embarrassing incident with Race Evans. She could just imagine Tom and Doug chortling when they heard about it. *So you need to make sure they never do.*

That was probably going to prove more difficult than changing her client's mind about firing Wallace. Mainly, she'd have to muzzle Frank. No doubt, he'd hear about her mistake—the man seemed to have a sixth sense for gossip—and would take great pleasure in retelling it. But she'd just have to use a bit of persuasion—such as threatening him with permanent security-desk detail if he ever shared the story.

THAT SAME EVENING, after Manning and several guests had gone to Santa Fe, Sheri was perched on a bar stool in the kitchen having a cup of coffee and listening to Cookie while he polished the countertops and complained, "I get so tired of these females flittin' around the boss, each one hoping to be Mrs. Manning Chandler. I especially hate it when they start invadin' my privacy.

"Miss Westin made chocolate-chip cookies 'for Manning,'" he said, mimicking Angela's high-pitched voice. "I wish she'd stay on that movie set, instead of running up here every time there's a break in shooting. It's one thing for the movie people to treat this place like a hotel, but Angela seems to think the Fort's her personal property."

From the guest files, Sheri knew that Angela was an actress. "Is she in the Race Evans film?"

"Yeah. Actually she's more interested in the boss than in acting. You might say she dabbles in it like she does cooking. The lady couldn't boil water when she got here, then all of a sudden she's Julia Child. She must have taken a crash course at the nearest cooking school when she saw how the boss is such a homebody."

Homebody? When she'd first come to the Fort, Sheri wouldn't have been able to fathom the description, but now that she reflected on it, the label *was* appropriate. Fort Tranquillity was Manning's home, and the employees his family. For the most part his social activities revolved around business, as he worked to make sure his clients were happy and entertained. The rest of the time, he seemed content to putter around the Fort. She began to wonder what kind of woman would fit into that picture. And why did she feel so inexplicably depressed knowing it wouldn't be a career woman who couldn't microwave popcorn without burning it? She was about to question Cookie further concerning Manning's homebody tendencies when she heard the man himself, and his guests, return. It was not yet ten.

Race Evans entered the kitchen. "Well, look who's here! My favorite secret agent." He pulled another stool up to the counter and sat down beside her, resting an arm—a bit too familiarly—on the back of her stool. Then he reached over to twist a strand of hair that had escaped from Sheri's ponytail. "Nice. I always did have a weakness for red hair."

Sheri ignored his comment, but got up and moved to the sink to rinse her coffee cup.

Race followed, propping a hip against the cabinet and toying with her hair again. "You should have joined us in town."

Before Sheri could tell Race that she hadn't been invited, Manning entered. "Better hit the sack, Race. You've got a big day ahead of you tomorrow." There was a hint of challenge in his voice.

Race nonchalantly stretched. "Didn't realize there was a curfew here, but I do have an early call in the morning." He turned to Sheri. "Well, good night, lovely Sheri." He kissed her quickly on the cheek, lingered a moment, then nuzzled her neck.

"Race." Manning's tone brooked no argument. "Hands off."

Race laughed. "Sorry, old pal. Didn't realize I was trespassing on private property." He headed for the door, giving Sheri a sly wink before disappearing.

Cookie had put away his cleaning gear and said good-night on Race's heels, leaving Sheri and Manning alone.

"Your interference wasn't necessary."

"You don't know Race Evans. Then again, maybe you want to. He's a big star—perhaps you liked the attention."

"It's not that. It's just that you probably have him thinking..." Sheri's face reddened in embarrassment.

"Thinking what?"

"I don't need your protection, Mr. Chandler."

Manning slipped his hands in the pockets of his jeans and leaned back, laughing. "Oh, is that what I was doing? Well, as the saying goes, turnabout's fair play." He laughed again. "Good night, lovely Sheri," he said, echoing Race's words as he walked out of the kitchen.

CHAPTER FOUR

SHERI WAS IN HER room preparing for bed and thinking about Manning. His behavior in the kitchen had unnerved her; he'd acted almost like a jealous suitor. But she decided that Manning was simply attempting to keep the hired help separate from the guests. Perhaps his method did seem a bit proprietary, but that didn't mean he was attracted to her. So why was she wishing he'd meant it when he called her "lovely Sheri"?

She went into the bathroom for a drink of water, trying to get her mind off Manning and back on her job, which was becoming more difficult every day. Still, it was hardly surprising that she'd be preoccupied with him. After all, the man was more than just good-looking; his charismatic presence attracted virtually every woman he met.

"And he's totally out of your league," she reminded herself aloud. Sheri couldn't imagine being Manning's date at one of those upper-crust social functions he attended. She definitely wasn't polo-club or charity-ball material. No, she was a working girl and, until now, proud of it. Why did she suddenly feel inferior? He wasn't better than she was, just the product of a different background.

However, when and if she decided to make room in her life for a man, he had to be someone she'd feel comfortable bringing to her tiny apartment in Houston, or taking to Tom's modest home. Not someone like Manning who was more accustomed to his father's River Oaks mansion or the exclusive New York town house owned by his mother—or, for that matter, the Fort. Someone who, if he got bored with those stateside locations, could always escape to the family's posh vacation hideaway on a beach in Barbados. Wallace Security might be growing, but it would be a long time before the three of them finished paying off loans and pumping income back into the business, a long time before the fantasy of the "good life" ever became a reality.

Why am I even worrying about it? she wondered. Despite the Mr. Macho routine with Race, Manning wasn't the slightest bit interested in her. Anyway, he had enough female attention to last ten men a lifetime. A new group of guests had arrived last night. She'd seen them unloading what looked to be a ton of luggage over at the cabanas. Sheri doubted that Manning would have time even to notice she was around. And if he did? Well, she'd make certain everything between them remained purely business. She had to; that was the only way to keep herself from these dangerous flights of fancy.

Sheri was frustrated at how poorly the investigation was going. She'd hoped the latest note and its connection with a Fort typewriter would enable her to break the case. But she had no idea whether the note had been typed last week or last year. She'd checked the ribbon as soon as she and Manning had returned from the camping trip and found that it was brand-new. And the typewriter was in an area to which almost everyone had access. Even if the agents had dusted for prints the day the message was typed, their list of suspects probably wouldn't have been any shorter. A staff member, a guest, a delivery person, *anybody* could have used that machine.

The next few days were tedious. Sheri went back to poring over the files until she almost had them memorized. Then she spent her time observing Manning and the gaggle of ever-present women clients. And while she watched, she did another about-face and reevaluated her opinion of him. He *was* a playboy, she decided. He flirted, he teased, he complimented. The way he cosseted those women was downright revolting.

A group of flight attendants had arrived from Denver that morning, two of them apparently old friends of Manning's. Unlike the other guests, these women had been given rooms in the main house, just down the hall from Sheri. Fortunately for Manning, Angela was off with the movie crew. Although the starlet shared meals in the main house and invited herself into Cookie's kitchen, she'd never been asked to stay at the headquarters. Sheri could imagine Angela's annoyance at having to share Manning with Mitzi Stevens and Jamie Harper.

Shortly before lunch, Sheri joined Manning and the guests. The brunette, Mitzi, was curled up in the corner of a sofa, knitting an afghan, while the blonde,

Jamie, sat on the patio painting the distant Sangre de Cristo Mountains.

"The name means 'blood of Christ,'" Manning said, leaning over Jamie's shoulder. The woman smiled at him, then playfully threatened his nose with the blob of green paint on the tip of her brush. He straightened and backed away, laughing, then crossed the room to talk to another female guest.

Manning stayed so busy flitting from woman to woman—like a human honey bee sampling the flowers, Sheri thought—that she wondered how he managed to do any training. Her eyes trailed after him as he made his rounds, his body-hugging navy T-shirt and white shorts both embossed with the Fort's logo, bringing admiring looks from women. *Show-off,* she muttered silently. *He knows he's a candidate for the sexiest man in America and he wants everyone else to notice, too.* And they obviously were.

That afternoon the crowd moved to the outside pool. Manning and Juan and a couple of other trainers were leading a water-aerobics class for a group of guests. Frank was watching from one end of the pool while Sheri sat at the other end, her feet dangling over the side. The tension she always felt around water was making her as nervous as the possibility that Wallace had become too lax about Manning's safety.

The class ended, and Manning walked over to join her. "Why don't you swim a few laps to cool off?"

"No, thanks," Sheri replied, taking her feet out of the water and inching backward on the deck. "I'm on duty." The mere suggestion that she get in the water increased her anxiety.

"Frank's on duty," he countered. "You're just afraid of getting your hair wet." Before she knew what was happening, he'd tossed her into the pool.

It happened so quickly that her only reaction was to let out a shriek as she flayed her arms frantically. Hitting the surface, she sank to the bottom, came up sputtering, then went under again. When she sank the third time, Manning dived in after her, pulled her first to the steps, then to the concrete deck. As everyone gathered around, he placed her on her stomach and straddled her, then began pounding her back.

"Get off me, you idiot," she gurgled, spewing water.

"Are you all right?"

"I'm fine. Just leave me alone." Sheri twisted away, then rose to her feet and walked unsteadily into the house, Manning following.

"Go back to your bathing beauties," she said as she wrung her hair with her hands. "There's a bunch of women out there who want your company."

Manning ignored her outburst. "Are you sure you're all right? That was a damn stupid thing for me to do."

"No argument there."

He helped her down the hall. They reached the door of her room, and Sheri went inside; again he followed. By now she was trembling, all self-control gone.

"You're shivering." He rubbed his hands vigorously up and down her arms.

Sheri lurched from his touch. "Please, spare me your concern." She shoved him toward the door. "Now go."

"No, I won't." He walked to the adjoining bath and pulled a terry-cloth spa robe from the hook behind the door. "Get out of that swimsuit and into this. I'll be right back."

"The door will be locked."

"If it is, I'll break the damned thing down."

Minutes later Manning returned with a snifter of brandy. "Drink this, then get into bed. Why the hell didn't you tell me you can't swim?"

"I can swim. You just caught me off guard."

"People who can swim generally do. When I tossed you into the pool, you sank to the bottom like a bowling ball."

"It was a fluke."

"I don't believe you. Talk, lady, and this time, tell me the truth." His hands were on Sheri's shoulders, pinning her against the bed.

"I said it was a fluke." Her voice was uneven, whispery. Manning was too close. She couldn't deal with the incident in the pool and with him, too. "Please leave."

Manning seemed ready to argue, but instead he eased off the bed. "I'll have Cookie send up a dinner tray, and we'll talk about this tomorrow."

The next day Manning had either decided to disregard the swimming incident or was sidetracked by the arrival of another letter, a note almost identical to the others he'd received—"Chandler will meet death. Soon."

"This doesn't make any sense at all," Sheri told Frank as the two sat in their small office studying the scrap of paper. "The messages are coming more frequently, but nothing else has happened."

Sheri would have liked to run a fingerprint check, but that would involve the police and the FBI. Manning still insisted that the authorities be kept out. Sheri didn't press the point, since she wasn't sure the police would find anything.

Sheri was convinced Manning had erred in suspecting a staff member, positive herself that the threats weren't coming from within. Her conclusion was based on a combination of detective work and intuition. She'd tried to put each of Manning's staff in the role of suspect, but none fit the profile of a kidnapper or extortionist or potential murderer. There was a strong camaraderie among the employees, with no loners or malcontents standing on the fringes.

She'd seldom seen a business where morale and job satisfaction were higher. But where did that leave Wallace in terms of suspects? She was sure there had to be more clues, an overlooked piece of evidence, maybe some kind of pattern.

"Most of the guests left this morning," Manning said as he entered the office. "And the new group won't be here until Monday. So, how about a day off, Sheri? We'll have lunch in town and do a little sightseeing."

"No way," Sheri responded. "It's too risky right now."

He shook his head. "You worry too much. Juan can come, too, if you want. Besides, if the culprit's someone here at the Fort, the danger's the same whether I stay in or go out. If it's a stranger, then it's about time we took the battle to him. I prefer to do something to force his hand, not play this waiting game. Otherwise, the harassment could go on forever.''

''I still don't think it's a good idea,'' Sheri said. She recalled reading in the local newspaper that this was the weekend for the annual Santa Fe Indian Market. There would be a mass of people viewing and purchasing the work of Indian artisans. It would be a security nightmare.

''But *I'm* calling the shots, remember? I'd like to leave before noon.''

By eleven, the group was gathered near the driveway, ready to climb into one of the Fort's minivans. Manning drove, and Juan sat in the front, which left the back seat to Sheri for the short trip into town. When they finally located a parking space in a lot several blocks from the square, Sheri was more concerned than ever. ''I think we should forget this. Manning, be realistic. If a kidnapper or an assassin happened to be part of this crowd, he could move around unnoticed.''

''I know, I know. We'll all be on guard. I just needed to get out. I was beginning to think I was in jail. And you...you haven't done any sight-seeing since you arrived. It's time you saw some of my favorite city.''

First, they visited the San Miguel Mission, constructed, according to Manning, during the reign of the Spanish in the early seventeenth century. From the mission, they walked to the Loretto Chapel where

Manning recited the history of the miraculous curved stairway.

"The chapel was almost finished when the sisters discovered there wasn't enough room for a conventional stairway to the choir loft. They prayed that a carpenter would come and solve their problem, and one day an old man appeared at the convent. With only hand tools, he built this wooden staircase. As you can see, it makes two complete turns and has no central support."

Sheri marveled at the construction and wondered how the wood could have been shaped into such a series of curves.

Manning continued his story. "After the stairs were done, the builder disappeared and was never heard from again. Was it St. Joseph or perhaps Christ himself? After all, both men were carpenters, and it's hard to believe a mere mortal built this masterpiece."

They left the chapel and strolled past the La Fonda Hotel to the plaza. "This was once the sight of bullfights, outdoor markets, even public floggings," commented Juan. "It's now on the Registry of Historic Places."

Near the Palace of the Governors, on the north side of the square, they stopped at one of the booths to admire the jewelry, and Manning bought a pair of dangling silver-and-turquoise earrings. He promptly handed them to Sheri.

"I can't accept these," she protested. "They're much too expensive."

"They match your outfit," he insisted, smiling. Sheri wore a Western-style skirt and blouse with a silver-link belt, one of the things she'd brought from Houston to help her blend in at the Fort. "You need a souvenir of your visit," Manning explained, obviously not about to let her refuse. "Consider it a bonus—a performance award."

His words took some of the joy out of the gift. For one thing, Sheri's performance hadn't been all that great. She'd strained her leg muscles jogging, screamed over a snake when they'd gone camping, attacked one of his most important guests and almost drowned, yet failed to come up with a single lead on their quarry. Some accomplishments.

The earrings were lovely, though, the type of gift a man would give a woman he cared about. But Manning probably tossed high-priced trinkets to so many women that the gesture was meaningless.

Pushing her misgivings aside, Sheri removed the earrings she wore, dropped them into her purse and replaced them with the new ones. They dangled to her shoulders and she couldn't help delighting in the way they felt when she moved her head. Manning Chandler was a dangerous man, she mused; he knew exactly how to enchant a woman. She'd have to be wary if she wanted to survive this assignment.

They continued wandering around the square, stopping occasionally at a booth. Manning bought two T-shirts, and Juan purchased a silver money clip with a bear claw etched into the metal. Sheri picked up a couple of postcards to mail to her brothers and one for her friend, Helen. She also told herself it was time to think of some gifts to take home. After all, the job here wouldn't last forever. Helen would like some

turquoise earrings, she decided, as she fingered Manning's gift.

At lunchtime, they ate a light meal in a restaurant
just off the plaza. Manning sat next to Sheri, his arm
resting casually across the back of her chair. Anyone
watching would assume she was his date. She, on the
other hand, knew the truth. She was his bodyguard,
his hired investigator. Her only goal for years had been
to gain respect in her profession. Why, then, did she
suddenly want something else, something more?

FOR THE NEXT THREE DAYS Sheri had the night shift.
Even though the Fort was peaceful, she felt as if she
were on an emotional seesaw. Not because of anything Manning did, but because of what he didn't do.
There were no fault findings, no midnight visits to the
detail room, certainly not any "lovely Sheri" remarks. She found herself missing the attention. She
was getting as bad as those other women Cookie had
complained about!

Manning was busy with the latest arrivals, especially one particular female guest, an actress who had
a cameo role in the Race Evans film. Manning treated
this visitor differently from everyone else. Her name
was Kimberly Conners, and she was the Fort's most
glamorous visitor to date.

Angela, too, was back. While friendly and effusive
to Kimberly's face, it was clear she viewed the woman
as major competition. And Sheri could understand
why. Kimberly Conners was beautiful. She was barely
over five feet, but had curves in all the right places.
Not to mention masses of shining blond hair. Yet, in-

stead of playing up her glamour, Kimberly spent most of her time in jeans and plaid shirts, or shorts and T-shirts.

Unfortunately for Angela and any other female who hoped to compete for a share of the limelight, the casual attire only served to accentuate Kimberly's natural beauty.

She and Manning seemed to be an item. They watched late movies on the VCR, took long walks together and swam in the heated outdoor pool in the moonlight. And, to drive a final nail in the coffins of the many aspiring Mrs. Manning Chandlers, Kimberly had the art of homemaking down pat.

She sewed, she crocheted, she cooked. And not just desserts. She prepared authentic New Mexico cuisine, such as green chile stew and blue corn tortillas. Even the normally territorial Cookie allowed her access to his kitchen. As opposed to Manning's other fans, whom the staff frequently regarded as nuisances, Kimberly was well thought of, even by Sheri. And like Angela, Sheri was miserably jealous.

She was surprised that she felt that way. Sheri didn't remember ever being jealous of anyone before, especially a woman. In her male-dominated existence, there had been many occasions when she'd envied men's opportunities. Jealousy of women, however, was something she didn't have time for.

She might as well admit—if only to herself—that she wanted to be one of the women Manning showered attention on, one of his privileged guests, instead of simply a hired hand. At the same time, she was determined Manning Chandler would never know of her misdirected longings.

Sheri began to realize how inexperienced and unworldly she was. Even if she did have a relationship with Manning, it wouldn't survive long. He would likely tire of her quickly and move on to someone more cosmopolitan, a woman who belonged in his social circle, his life. There was a lesson to be learned here. After she returned to Houston, perhaps she should be more open to her friends' and brothers' attempts at matchmaking.

It was after midnight. Sheri had just completed a routine check of the house, confirming that the alarms were set. Now she was curled up in a chair in the detail room with a new novel when Manning appeared. Sheri certainly hadn't expected to see him. She could feel a glow of pleasure heat her cheeks and wondered whether her reaction was evident to Manning. She kept her eyes on the book, hoping he wouldn't detect the tinge of pink. But her happiness was soon stifled as she remembered Kimberly. Had she been upset when he arose and left her bed?

"Still reading?"

She waited a moment, as though absorbed, before she looked up from her latest mystery and nodded. Manning was in his familiar navy bathrobe, his tanned muscular calves drawing her attention in spite of herself.

"I brought you a present." He handed her a couple of books. "You read too much cloak-and-dagger stuff."

Sheri scanned the covers. "Romances?" What was Manning Chandler expecting to achieve with this selection of reading material?

He smiled. "If you're going to escape from real life with fantasies, these will be much more beneficial than whodunits."

"Beneficial to whom?"

"Give them a try. Then we'll see if you've learned anything." He winked then, as if to punctuate his remark.

"No, *we* won't." She decided to call his bluff, to verbalize her thoughts. "What are you up to, Chandler?"

"Maybe I've sensed a spark between us."

"Sure of yourself, aren't you? But mistaken," she said, hoping she'd managed to make the protest sound convincing.

"You're only denying it because it scares you." He leaned over and raised her chin with his finger. "I've definitely found something Sheri Lindsey is afraid of. Commitment scares you, doesn't it?"

"That's ridiculous. I'm committed to any number of things," she replied, purposely misinterpreting his words.

"Being devoted to the job isn't what I'm talking about. But then again, it's less hazardous than personal involvement."

"I don't understand why you've come here bearing gifts." She picked up one of the romances and shook it at him. "And trying to psychoanalyze me. It would seem that your life and your bed are full enough at the moment."

"You sound like a jealous girlfriend," he mocked.

"Don't be ridiculous!"

Manning cocked his head. "I think you're wondering whether Kimberly and I are sleeping together." Now he laughed, a deep husky laugh. "You're jealous, all right. But, lovely Sheri, do you honestly believe I'd be out here if I had another woman waiting in my bedroom?"

"I don't know you well enough to predict your behavior."

"Still, you've got an overactive imagination if you think I bed every attractive woman who comes to the Fort. To tell the truth, though, fending off the women does get a little boring."

"Poor, poor man."

"I didn't mean to sound conceited. If they're attracted to me, the appeal is probably Chandler money, not Chandler the man. Kimberly's different. She likes me for me. But she's just a pal and a client."

Sheri studied him skeptically. Surely he couldn't be serious—women after him just for his money? Hardly. Hadn't the man looked in the mirror lately? And it was difficult to swallow the idea that the luscious Kimberly was only a friend. Sheri remained unconvinced, and she involuntarily glanced through the open door to the hallway, which led to Manning's suite.

"Four bedrooms over there, you know—mine and three guest rooms. Want to come see for yourself?"

Sheri shook her head.

"I insist you inspect them. It's the only way you're going to believe me." He took Sheri by the hand and pulled her to her feet.

She stood her ground and refused to budge. She wasn't about to go to his suite. Especially not with him in the grip of this devilish mood.

"Okay, have it your own way," he said, and left the room.

She sat back down and began leafing through one of the romance novels he'd given her.

Five minutes passed before he reappeared. "Did you hear that noise?"

Sheri looked up suspiciously. "What noise?"

He cupped his hand to his ear. "It seems to be gone now, but I'm sure I heard something. You'd better come and investigate. It may be a burglar. Or maybe our mysterious note sender has come to steal me away in the middle of the night."

"Don't be silly."

"Me, silly? This is serious. Do I need to yell and wake up the entire household, or are you going to check things out?"

"Oh, all right," Sheri said. She might as well indulge Manning. He obviously wasn't going to leave her alone until she did. She took out her service revolver and pushed Manning behind her, intending to play this for all it was worth.

"I don't think you'll need that." Manning had apparently forgotten his previous order about carrying a weapon. "It's probably just a mouse."

"Or a rat," Sheri said, ignoring his mischievous tone.

"That's Kimberly's room." Manning pointed to the first door they passed. "My bedroom's at the end of the hall."

Sheri swung open the last door with Manning on her heels. She could almost feel his breath on the back of her neck. She stepped inside and looked around. Manning tiptoed in after her.

The room, like the rest of the hacienda, was decorated in a Southwestern fashion, with rounded beams and a kiva fireplace in the corner. The massive king-size bed with its carved headboard dominated the space. Roughly finished furniture and an abundance of cacti in huge terra-cotta pots were skillfully arranged about the room. Manning had obviously been reading in bed. The brown satin sheets were thrown back, and there was an open book near the pillows.

Sheri dutifully looked under the bed, in the closets, checked the window locks, then inspected the bathroom, which was almost as big as the bedroom.

He watched her as she searched, grinning whenever she glanced his way. "Seems okay to me," she said. "Well, good night." She turned to leave.

He quickly moved between her and the door. "Stay and keep me company. I might hear the noise again."

"Really now. This is going too far. I've had enough of your fun and games."

He folded his arms across his chest. "Why are you so averse to fun and games? You know what they say about all work and no play." He was still grinning.

The light dancing in his eyes and the expression on his face were utterly appealing to her—and equally frustrating. "You're being childish."

"That's strange." Manning's expression sobered. "Because I don't feel a bit childish." He stepped closer to her, until mere inches separated them. "So, how about visiting for a while?" His lips started toward hers.

Sheri turned her head, her heart pounding furiously. She'd missed these encounters with Manning, missed the challenge of their sparring, missed the sexual tension. She wanted to stay, to give in to temptation. But she had to remember that she was at Fort Tranquillity to work, not to have a fling. He was still indulging in some sort of game, she reminded herself, and her earlier admonitions that he was off-limits echoed in her mind. Her resolve strengthened, she pulled away. "I'm sorry, but... I'm sorry." She left Manning's room and hurried back to the detail room.

"CONCENTRATE ON THE JOB, concentrate on the job." Sheri repeated the words over and over while she dressed the next afternoon, after sleeping the morning away. Her assignment at the Fort seemed unreal—like a daydream. True, there *was* a threat against Manning Chandler; she'd seen the notes, dug through the scant evidence. But it was as if someone merely wanted to keep him off balance, not harm him. So far—thank heaven—no acts of violence had occurred.

Sheri was determined to continue the investigation methodically, the way she worked best. She would discuss the approach with her brothers, then begin looking over the guest lists again to see if she could find a correlation between any guest's visits and the appearance of the notes. She'd also call Anson in Albuquerque and ask him to send another agent to the Fort without Manning's or anyone else's knowledge. Perhaps an undercover person might help break the case.

Once those arrangements were made, Sheri started to feel more composed. She needed to stay busy, she told herself, to stop her unproductive thoughts about Manning and resist his damnable appeal.

One more item remained on her agenda. A major item. She was going to conquer her fear of water, or drown trying. As much as she hated to admit it, many of Manning's accusations about Wallace security had been true. The agents weren't adequately trained when it came to physical skills and stamina. And that included her.

Running marathons didn't excuse her quaking at the mention of white-water rafting—or anything else a client wanted to do. And she vowed never to be in that position again. First, she'd complete her personal training regimen, then she'd decide what needed to be done about the rest of the agents.

Sheri put together a swimming schedule and attacked it like a training program. She headed for the pool early each morning before anyone else was stirring and returned in late evening for a brief swim. Her fears hadn't completely dissipated, but with each session, she gained more confidence. She even began to welcome the company that joined her after the first morning. Sometimes it was Frank or Juan, and once even Cookie showed up to swim laps with her.

She'd been training for a week when she arrived at the pool one morning to find Manning there, standing waist deep in the water. Sheri wore a pale pink maillot, and she felt Manning's appraising eye as she self-consciously made her way to the pool. If she hadn't seen all the female pulchritude around the Fort, she'd have said his gaze was an approving one. But when you faced movie-star competition in hankie-size bits of material that passed for swimsuits, such speculation was ridiculous.

Sheri sat down on the edge of the pool and nervously dangled her legs over the side. She wished Manning weren't there. Her uneasiness had nothing to do with her fear of water but with the nearness of a man she could barely resist. Hoping to maintain her composure, she took several deep slow breaths.

Manning swam toward her. "That's a good start. Now give me your hand and I'll help you in."

"No, I don't think so."

Manning pushed his fingers through his damp hair. "Okay, tell you what. Just put your arms around my neck, and I'll hold you up."

"I don't need anyone to hold me up." She left her perch, walked to the diving board, then defiantly executed a perfect jackknife into the pool.

When she surfaced, Manning was treading water by her side. "Brave girl—most of the time." He wrapped his arms around her waist and pulled her to him.

"Manning, don't." She struggled to break away, but he held her fast.

"I'm proud of you," he said, gazing steadily into her eyes. "It takes a rare person to recognize a fear and conquer it."

"I knew I hadn't fooled you," Sheri said, trying to ignore the feel of his arms as she steered the conversation to a less personal tone. "By the way, I appreciate all the partners you've sent to play lifeguard for me."

"It isn't wise for anyone to swim alone, regardless of ability."

"Well, everybody can relax now. I think I've finally overcome my fear. I guess I'll be able to sleep at night without worrying about rapids in my future." She looked up at him. "When do you plan the rafting trip?"

He didn't answer for a few moments, but gently stroked her cheek with the back of his hand. When he did speak, it wasn't to answer her question. "I'm the one with trouble sleeping now."

"Oh?"

"I lie awake nights thinking about you." His fingers traced a path across her collarbone, causing a flush of warmth to spread through Sheri's body. Then his hands dropped to her waist.

In a gesture that felt completely natural, Sheri slid her hands up his arms and clasped them behind his neck. Her eyes fluttered closed as she anticipated his kiss. This time he didn't disappoint her.

Sheri could almost imagine the droplets of water on her face turning to steam as he pressed his body tightly against hers. Then suddenly, inexplicably, Manning pulled away from her. Sheri's eyes flew open and her hands gripped the side of the pool to keep her balance. His back was to her, but she could tell that he was as affected by their kiss as she had been. After long moments, he plunged beneath the water. She watched while he swam laps as if he was being chased. Finally he stopped and hoisted himself out of the pool. He grabbed a towel from a nearby chair and walked over to Sheri, who still clung to the pool's edge. He extended a hand to help her from the water. "We'd better go in."

Sheri allowed herself to be pulled out, then retrieved her own towel. She dabbed at her face, using the towel as a shield to cover the hurt and confusion she felt.

THAT EVENING when Sheri appeared for her swim, it was Juan who met her. "The boss had to go into town. Frank asked me to tell you he was tagging along."

Sheri treaded water for a few minutes and then did a couple of feeble laps before climbing out of the pool and heading back to her room. Now that she reflected on it, Manning had been avoiding her all day. He obviously regretted the morning's aquatic interlude. Just as obviously, he didn't think he owed her an explanation.

Being abandoned like this made Sheri feel even more rejected. If he thought he'd made a mistake, all he had to do was say so. To kiss and run was almost cowardly, and Sheri experienced a sense of disillusionment when she realized that her fantasy man was all too human.

But if that was the way he wanted it, she had to put her emotions—and the incident—behind her. She hoped Manning wouldn't let it destroy their business relationship. If he displayed any standoffishness, everyone would not only notice, but speculate on the change in his behavior.

So far, she'd managed to keep her infatuation with Manning Chandler a secret. She didn't want to become an object of gossip for Frank or any of Manning's staffers. Or, even worse, her brothers. Especially now that she felt so disenchanted. Manning's message had been loud and clear—he enjoyed the chase, but he didn't want to risk getting caught. She'd have to tell the man to stop worrying. Unlike all the other women at the Fort, Sheri Lindsey was not out to snare him—at least not any longer.

CHAPTER FIVE

"HE'S AT IT AGAIN," Frank groaned as he entered the detail room. "I should have known it was too good to last. I'd just started to relax, deciding Chandler had given up on the maneuvers because of your being here. But that turned out to be wishful thinking. The man's driven. That's what he is, driven." He picked up the calendar and began calculating. "I can't believe it's another twenty years before I can even consider retiring."

Sheri had become used to Frank's constant griping, but he seemed more agitated than usual. And when Frank became agitated, his chauvinism came to the fore. His remark about Manning's giving up his more strenuous activities on her account irritated her. On the other hand, she had to agree that life at the Fort had been rather tame recently, and she perked up at the thought that something challenging was in the works. "What's the deal?" she asked.

"Rappelling, that's what! Manning's trying to be another Arnold Schwarzenegger. He wants to promote outdoor adventures and introduce survival training. He's determined to give the program a run-through. I guess that means we're part of the action."

"I hope so," Sheri said.

"Have you lost your mind, too?"

"No, but don't forget our job is to stick with the client, come hell or high water. And speaking of water, I thought rafting was on the agenda."

"Oh, don't worry, it is, *after* the rappelling." Frank leaned against a corner of the desk. "We won't get a moment's rest, unless we're lucky enough to get killed on the mountainside."

Despite her concerns, Sheri couldn't help smiling. "We should have known the serenity of the past few weeks wouldn't last forever. 'Fess up, partner—wasn't all that peace and quiet beginning to get to you?"

"Well..." He sighed.

She plucked the calendar out of his hand and returned it to the desk. "Now, no more retirement talk. Where are we going and when?"

"An overnight trip to some cliffs in southern Colorado this week—he hasn't found a closer place he likes yet," Frank said. "After that, we're back at the Fort for a couple of days before trotting off to run the rapids. Chandler's supposed to give us a schedule this afternoon."

Sheri shook her head. "He does seem to be flaunting his fearlessness, doesn't he? But at least there haven't been any more threats."

"Oh. I thought you knew. Another one came early today. That's probably what made him decide about the trip."

"Well, that changes everything. He's just going to have to undecide." Sheri rose from her chair. "I'm not about to be part of some suicide mission. Just because nothing's happened so far doesn't mean nothing will." And she was sure something *was* going to happen.

Before Wallace Security had been called in, there had been only three warnings, each coming a month apart, and the frequency had remained the same when the first Wallace crew came on the scene. Now, notes were arriving every few days. She needed to check this latest one. Had it also been typed on the machine at the Fort? She rushed down the stairs and into Manning's office, arriving to find him on the telephone rattling off a supply order.

"Check everyone's size for rock-climbing boots, then we'll need rope, first-aid supplies, plenty of high-energy food. I'll make a list." His voice was animated, enthusiastic.

She bided her time, allowing Manning to finish his conversation and hang up the phone. "I can't believe you actually plan to do something as dangerous as this," she scolded when he finally replaced the receiver. "Not after getting another warning."

Manning showed no hint of being intimidated. Instead, his face hardened into a determined scowl. "That's part of the reason I *am* doing it. I'll be damned if I'll cower in the Fort like it's some kind of bunker. If this idiot wants to take me on, then he can go right ahead. But I won't be unprepared. Juan and Cookie will be along. I know I can trust them. I've hired your group, and you can call in a couple of reinforcements if you want. Do whatever you think is necessary. But we *are* going."

"I insist—"

He cut her off. "Forget it." Then his voice softened. "Sheri, listen. I've been thinking about this a lot. Threats, kidnapping, terrorism, all those kinds of crimes, are worldwide concerns. Not only for businesspeople, but for government officials and tourists, too. In order to protect themselves, a lot of people are taking training. Survival schools are cropping up everywhere. And that would be a natural extension of what I'm already doing here. Consider this a perfect opportunity for a trial run."

"Wrong. Perfect opportunities don't involve potential danger. Why would you even consider something like this? You seem to have all the business you need. Even more important, why take it on now? What's the rush?"

"I've got someone who's interested in the kind of training we've been talking about. I need to test a few ideas before I meet with him next week. Besides, I'm tired of being pushed around by some coward who sends unsigned messages." He picked up the letter and waved it in the air as he spoke. "So, whether I have the approval of Wallace Security or not, I'm going to do this. If you don't want to come..."

"You know better than that." She sighed. "I'd better start making arrangements." Sheri got to the door, then turned back to retrieve the note from Manning. "I'll just hang on to this." Manning might have a cavalier attitude about the possibility of harm, but that didn't mean she had to have one.

In her own office, Sheri studied the newest note. The type was different, so she dismissed that angle. The note could still have been typed at the Fort; after all, there were at least half a dozen other machines around, plus several word processors. She examined the note again and finally determined that a typewriter had definitely been used. Not that it mattered. The note could have been written anytime, anywhere. The equipment was irrelevant, she decided. Better to focus her energies elsewhere.

The wording was the same, yet nothing in the sparse death threat provided a clue. Her fears about the outing intensified. Previously the notes had come only when there was a large group of guests at the Fort, which had convinced her that one of them was their note sender. But now the theory had been undermined because this past week had been a "down time"—a time when no clients were at the Fort—which, according to Cookie, Manning periodically scheduled as a break for the staff. So, either they were wrong about the perpetrator's being a guest, or he'd changed his approach.

Regardless, Sheri felt as if they were back to square one, perhaps even off the board completely. And it was still possible that the culprit might be a staff member, because this new message, like all the others, had a Santa Fe postmark.

Sheri pondered Manning's taking the offensive. Occasionally she approved of that sort of activity and had even suggested it herself in cases where the investigation had been stymied. Now, she wasn't sure. What if something happened to Manning on the trip? She recognized that her fear for his safety went beyond the usual concerns. This time she was actually terrified that he'd be hurt. This time she was personally involved.

She had grown to care about Manning Chandler, infuriating though he could be. Just like all those other gullible females, she had succumbed to his charm. Despite her belief that she didn't belong in his world, she found him impossible to resist.

THE NEXT AFTERNOON, Juan and Frank were at the top of a two-hundred-foot mesa not far from Durango, Colorado. Cookie and Sheri were at the bottom, binoculars in hand, watching the initial descent of Manning and two other Fort employees who'd never rappelled before. Juan, who'd had some experience rappelling when he was in the military, would follow them down, leaving Frank to stand guard where he was.

They'd spent the morning going through rudimentary lessons in rock climbing and doing a little bouldering, which Manning explained as "climbing around some rocks you can't possibly tumble off." Then he added, "Later on we'll do some serious climbing, but for that, I want to bring in a few experts. What we're doing now is elementary stuff."

Sheri found herself enjoying the day—the mountain air, crisp with a hint of autumn, the occasional glimpses of deer and other wildlife. Even the higher altitude was causing her no problems. She felt surprisingly free and unfettered.

But worry kept returning, despite Manning's assurances that the risks were minimal. Out here, menace came from both man and nature. Rappelling was one of the most dangerous sports—if one could even call it a sport. A little slip of the hands, a frayed rope, a sudden gust of wind was all it would take.... The thought sent shivers down her spine.

And Manning was an obvious target to someone with a high-powered rifle. That frightening image made her shiver again. Was there actually a business deal in the offing as Manning alleged, or had he insisted on these risky outings because he experienced some kind of satisfaction from living on the edge?

Sheri's interest in Manning's motives was more than clinical musing, since she herself had been accused of being too adventuresome for her own good. It was an unfair accusation as far as she was concerned; however, if Tom and Doug hadn't been such consummate watchdogs, Sheri probably would have given in to a few of her more daring impulses.

She pushed back the brim of her baseball cap to get a better view of the activity. The men looked so vulnerable hanging on the cliffside that any enthusiasm she might have had about the venture was curbed by renewed concern. She noted the surveillance helicopter parked above, the one she had insisted on.

Manning would be the first one to reach the bottom. Sheri watched as he continued his descent. He was dressed like the rest of the group—denim shorts, T-shirt and special rock-climbing shoes. On the other men, the attire revealed a slight paunch here or knobby knees there, but on Manning the outfit served only to display his rugged handsomeness.

She monitored his movements through the binoculars, her gaze fixed on the placement of his hands and how he used his feet to propel himself away from the rocks. He made descending the cliff look effortless.

The two beginners were sandwiched between Manning and Juan. There were a few uneasy moments and a bit of cajoling by Manning until each staffer touched his feet on the solid ground and smiled triumphantly. Finally it was Juan's turn. His descent was fast and efficient.

"That's enough for today, don't you think?" Manning's question was directed at Sheri, who gave him a nod, and then waved to Frank. Soon he and the helicopter crew had joined the assembly below.

Sheri returned to the campsite with a sense of elation. They'd made it through the first day. Perhaps her anxiety about the trip was unnecessary. After all, they'd carefully checked the equipment to ensure no one had tampered with any of it. And the helicopter crew was responsible for extended ground surveillance, but hadn't reported any unusual movement in the area. Still, it was a relief that the risky activities were temporarily finished.

That night the group camped out under the stars, their tents in a semicircle by the edge of a small bubbling stream. Sheri was developing a new appreciation for camping, for the brief escape from civilization and the fellowship of the camp fire. She'd grown to like the sights and sounds of the country.

Most of the time the stars were hardly visible over Houston, but here, they speckled the cloudless blue-black sky. Sheri rolled an extra sweater into a ball and lay back against it, studying the panorama above her.

"Beautiful," Manning said.

"It is, isn't it?"

"I wasn't talking about the sky. I was thinking of something much, much closer." Manning's eyes were fixed on her, and Sheri couldn't prevent a flush of pleasure.

She sat up. "Did you enjoy your thrills and chills today?" she joked, trying to maintain control over her body and divert his attention at the same time.

"I thought it went well, but I'm not averse to a few more thrills and chills." He took her hand.

Sheri jerked it away, annoyed at his teasing. "Go bother Frank."

"I doubt he'd appreciate my holding his hand. No, moonlight requires a pretty woman."

"Too bad there isn't one around."

"Fishing for compliments, Sheri? I hardly believe that's necessary. I'm sure you hear lots of sweet nothings from your male co-workers."

"I don't listen. I make it a point not to get involved with male co-workers—or clients. So you'd better get back to your tent. I'm going to go to mine and get some sleep." She rose and purposefully walked toward her tent.

"I'd much rather be with you."

His soft words were almost her undoing. She realized how much she wanted him to mean them, and that thought only made her more resentful. She stopped and slowly turned to face him. "I'd be flattered if I didn't know you're focusing all your attention on me simply because I'm the only female within twenty miles."

"Unfair. I pay attention to you even when there are other women around."

"Forget it, Chandler. I'm not your type."

"Is that something else you've figured out about me—my type? Pray tell, describe the ideal Manning Chandler female."

"Okay." Sheri moved closer, deciding that her best defense against the feelings Manning aroused in her was to irritate him. "Obviously you're not going away." She held up her fingers and began counting off points. "First, she's tiny. None of the women who interest you is taller than five three. Apparently you like to dominate your women in more ways than one." She took a step closer to him.

"Second, she's a homebody. No career woman for you. That's how you resist permanent arrangements with the starlets. You want an old-fashioned traditional helpmate. And, despite their best efforts, none of them has convinced you she fits the mold." Sheri knew she had no basis for what she was saying other than one of Cookie's comments, but Manning did seem to appreciate Kimberly's meals and craft work. And there had to be some reason Angela had been trying her hand in the kitchen.

"You'd probably prefer a wife who stays pregnant all the time," Sheri continued, "and presents you with a lot of little Chandlers, including a Manning V. Also, you'd want her wearing an apron and either handing you home-baked goodies or a cocktail when you walked in the door."

Manning snorted. "That's ridiculous. I know you're trying to make some sort of point with your exaggerations, but there's a helluva lot to say for a woman who puts her family and the man in her life first.''

Sheri ignored the indignation in his tone and resumed her list. "Third, she's domesticated." She smiled at her play on words. "A woman who'll let you do her talking and thinking, who'll consider you lord and master. She'll be tamed, subservient.''

Manning laughed and raised an eyebrow. "That's not necessarily true. I wouldn't mind a wild filly. It might be fun taming her myself." His expression told Sheri to whom he was referring.

"Are you sure you don't mean break?"

"Who'd want a broken woman?" He moved toward her. Even if she couldn't see him in the starlight, Sheri would have felt his presence.

Her tent and sleeping bag were at one end of the semicircle. Sheri had intentionally set up there to give herself more privacy. Now she regretted her decision. Most of the group were already sleeping, worn out from their strenuous activity. Frank, his ankle almost completely healed, was sharing guard duty with one of Manning's trainers, but they'd already passed the encampment and were at least fifty yards away.

Manning seemed to sense her fear. "Is that panicky look in your eyes because I'm too near, or because you're thinking about the possibility of a snake slithering toward the campsite?"

The word "snake" made Sheri forget all about Manning's advances. "Should I be closer to the fire?"

"You're probably closer than you realize." The moonlight made his eyes glimmer almost wickedly. "Yeah, I think the taming of Sheri might be quite a challenge." He ran his thumb over her bottom lip. "See you tomorrow, lovely Sheri." His voice was so gentle it was like a caress.

Tame me? Wild filly? mused Sheri as he walked away. Who did he think he was? Pompous jackass seemed a good description. Yet that self-assurance was part of Manning's appeal. He knew who he was and what people felt about him. Much as she'd tried to disguise her own reactions, he probably even knew what Sheri felt.

And there was no denying that she *was* attracted to him. She did feel a tingle of excitement when he was near, her heart did react in that crazy unfamiliar way whenever he said "lovely Sheri." Particularly when he sounded sincere, as he had just now. Gone were all traces of the sarcasm he'd used when mimicking Race Evans. *Get hold of yourself, Sheri. The man's only toying with you. Remember, Manning Chandler IV has no real interest in Sheri Lindsey from Wallace Security.* She had to keep reminding herself of that.... Oh, well, maybe it would keep her thoughts off snakes.

Cookie served a feast the next morning—crisp strips of bacon, banana-walnut pancakes with maple syrup, and lots of strong hot coffee. The cool mountain air was exhilarating after the summer heat, and Sheri and Frank enthusiastically pitched in to help Manning's staff break camp. Today, they would rappel for several more hours before they started back for the Fort around noon. Even Sheri would try. It was a good thing Tom and Doug didn't know about her participation in the runs, or else they would have become protective again and attempted to stop the trip, or at least prevent her from going.

Sheri herself was having second thoughts about making a descent. As she fastened the harness and listened to Manning's instructions about the ropes, she grew even more apprehensive. It had been hard enough watching everyone else, and now it was her turn.

She would be dropping quickly, with only her strength and her skill keeping her from plummeting to the bottom. She tried to recall the lessons Manning had given back at the Fort. Practice and reality were far apart, she decided, as she glanced nervously at the small figures of Cookie and the others on the ground below.

"Don't look down," Manning admonished. "Just concentrate on what you're doing, and you'll be fine."

He was right, Sheri told herself, then began her descent. She'd be fine. Besides, this was exactly what she wanted, to be treated as an equal and allowed to do her job the same as any man—even if it meant rappelling down this intimidating mountain.

Manning seemed to have gained faith in her abilities. He stayed at the top and simply shouted instructions as her boots rebounded from the cliffside and her hands slid along the rope. When her rappel was finally over, she felt a wave of satisfaction, her self-confidence soaring.

The other descents were going well, too. Juan's rope snagged halfway down, causing everyone to watch apprehensively as he worked to free himself, but that was the only tense moment. The Fort Tranquillity staff was in such good physical shape that the new maneuvers were going flawlessly, putting everyone in high spirits. Until Manning's turn.

He had just started his final descent when several large rocks broke loose and rained down on him, battering his arms and head. It happened so fast that Sheri could only stare mutely as Manning let go of the rope and began to fall. She felt as though her heart would explode as he dropped almost fifteen feet before righting himself and grabbing the line.

Frank peered anxiously over the edge and called out, "Are you all right?" In response, Manning waved, then continued rappelling. Sheri folded her arms around her body, shivering as if the temperature was subzero instead of in the mid-seventies. Manning could have died. The thought brought tears to her eyes, but she angrily brushed them away. She rarely cried and wasn't about to start blubbering over Manning Chandler.

When he reached the bottom, the group hurried over to him. "Good Lord," Cookie said, "you gave us a scare. You sure you're okay?"

"Yeah," he said. "Except I seem to have a slight headache." His fingers went up to a bloodied place on his forehead that he dabbed at with the back of his hand until Sheri passed him a tissue. She was trying desperately to behave like a concerned security agent, trying to hide her joy that he was safe, trying to stop herself from hugging him tightly to her.

Juan went for the first-aid kit while Sheri inspected Manning's forehead and several abrasions on his arm.

"You could have been killed," she chastised, her voice wavering a bit though she struggled to keep it even.

"Careful, Agent Lindsey, you almost sound like you care." He snapped his fingers. "Oh, yes, I forgot. You're my bodyguard. It'd be a poor career move to lose me."

His sarcasm stung, and again she had to fight back tears. "Don't you realize that you were falling? You came close to serious injury. Or... or worse!"

"I guess an accident would look almost as bad on your record as the bad guy doing me in." He laughed, clearly trying to diffuse the tension.

Sheri sighed. The man was impossible. Obviously Manning wasn't taking this incident any more seriously than he did the others. *Oh, well, if you can't beat 'em, join 'em,* she decided as she shrugged in a "who knows?" gesture. "It'd be a toss-up," she said. "Actually there's probably more reason to fear that you'll be done in by a disgruntled Wallace staffer than by our crazy correspondent."

"Glad to see you've finally found a sense of humor about this fiasco. You know, you're even more beautiful when you smile." The look he gave her made Sheri feel exposed, as though he'd kissed her in full view of the rest of the group. She moved away, angry at herself for caring too much, and at Manning Chandler for caring too little.

Sheri insisted that Manning return to the Fort by helicopter with her, while the others followed on the ground. As soon as the helicopter landed at the Fort, Manning started planning for his next adventure.

"This is exactly what I've been complaining about," Frank told Sheri as the two sat in their office the next afternoon. "I'm sure you haven't appreciated my comments, but now it ought to be clear what a nightmare it is to chase after him."

Sheri shook her head in dismay. "It's crystal clear. I'm just glad the rappelling came off as well as it did."

"Sure, the rappelling went okay. I even had some regrets because my ankle kept me from trying. But the rest of Wallace would have been a disaster here. Pete Garcia would have had an anxiety attack, since he's afraid of heights, and Anson would have gone down like a sandbag off a ledge. I, for one, am hoping Wallace doesn't bother renewing our contract with Chandler."

"If he even *wants* to renew," Sheri said. "After all, we're only around because of some ominous notes. When this situation is resolved, I can't see our being needed anymore. In case you've forgotten, our client has been none too happy with our services."

"Is this the kind of gig I can expect from the company—this rah-rah outdoor adventure stuff? If so, I may want to consider other lines of security work."

Frank had begun griping again, and Sheri's patience was waning. "Do you intend to sit around office lobbies for the rest of your life, Frank?"

"I've never been assigned to lobbies, and I don't plan to start. But I wouldn't mind a cushy job such as keeping an eye on some ladies, especially lookers like the ones who visit the Fort. That's my idea of a perfect assignment—not hurtling my body over the edge of a cliff.'' Frank lapsed into silence, obviously day-dreaming about ideal jobs.

Sheri shook her head as she walked away, searching for a cup of coffee and an escape from Frank. Manning had finally settled down and was in his room resting, so she had time to herself. She moved to the patio, where she sat alone, contemplating her future. A future that no longer seemed predictable—not since this experience in New Mexico.

She'd been content at Wallace Security, but was it time to sell her share to her brothers and go on to something else? That notion didn't appeal to her. Yet neither did returning to the existence she'd had before coming to Fort Tranquillity.

Perhaps it was normal to get an occasional attack of "What am I going to do with the rest of my life?" Still, she recognized that she needed something different, something that would challenge her—*but something that involves Manning,* a small voice within her said. Sheri idly tapped a fingernail against the surface of the glass patio table, trying to ignore that voice.

Better to think about business. Since coming to Santa Fe she'd learned that Manning was right—the Wallace agents didn't have the background for the kind of protection work needed at the Fort, for the kind of expansion she and her brothers had talked about. Wallace Security was unprepared.

How could she change that? The seeds of an idea started to take hold. She, Tom and Doug had concentrated on building a business and had forgotten an essential ingredient—continuing education. They needed to upgrade their employees' abilities, not just hire more of them. She went inside to phone her brothers.

"I don't know, Sheri. The troops wouldn't be excited about such a prospect, that's for sure. I doubt we can bribe any of them to work with Chandler on a project like that."

"Tom, you've dreamed for years about having an elite international protection firm. I've shared those dreams, but I don't believe they can be achieved without refocusing some of our efforts. Yes, Chandler can be a pain in the neck, but he also has a top-notch facility. A facility that would make a perfect training site for Wallace Security. I'd like to approach him about a joint venture once we get this other situation cleared up. What do you say?"

"Let me give him a call."

"That won't be necessary. I can take care of this."

"I'd feel better if I talked to Chandler."

When Sheri hung up the phone, she felt frustrated by Tom's interference. It was all her fault. She should have gone ahead and acted on her instinct instead of running the idea by her brothers. After all, she'd thought of it; she didn't need them to make it a reality.

Later that afternoon Manning stopped her in the hallway. "I talked to Houston."

"Oh?"

"I think your concept for training Wallace agents here is an excellent idea, and I'm excited about what we can do. I want to complete the rafting trip, then we'll sit down and put together a training regimen." He put a hand on her shoulder. "This is a promise—

when we get through with your agents, no one, and that includes me, will be able to accuse them of being inept."

Sheri took in what he was saying with a feeling of shock and pleasure. First, Tom had told Manning it was her proposal. Second, Manning was enthusiastic. Would wonders never cease? It appeared all these men had finally entered the modern world!

"A partnership between us has a lot of potential," Manning continued. "For one thing, we can steer clients to each other. And that's only a small item. Tom's coming here in a couple of weeks to help us brainstorm, and then we can work out the logistics."

Sheri's momentary high faded abruptly. Her brother might have given her credit, but he was rushing out to oversee the details himself. *Oh, well, he does handle most of the contracts,* she rationalized.

"Uh, by the way, do you and your partner have some kind of special relationship?"

Despite his casualness, Sheri sensed an underlying tension in Manning, almost an anger. "What makes you ask that?"

"The guy seems unusually interested in your comings and goings."

"The guy, as you put it, has a wife, two little children and a third on the way."

"That doesn't answer my question." Manning jammed a hand into the pocket of his shorts, jingling a few loose coins while he waited for her response.

"As far as I'm concerned it does," Sheri retorted, then managed to calm down. No need to snap at Manning just because she was upset with Tom. "I don't date married men, but for your information, this one happens to be my brother."

"Wallace, Lindsey. I didn't realize you were married. Or are you divorced?"

"Neither. Technically he's a half brother, although we've never cared much for technicalities."

"I didn't know. Tom and Doug are nice guys."

"Most of the time," Sheri agreed.

She talked to her brothers again that night, first briefing them on the investigation, then discussing the potential contract. Their heartfelt congratulations on the training proposal soothed her ruffled feathers. But being Tom and Doug, they couldn't leave well enough alone.

"I'm not sure you should be out there with Chandler any longer," Doug said. "He's behaving himself, isn't he? He hasn't made any passes?"

Sheri dodged the questions with one of her own. "When would he get around to me, even if he wanted to? There are busloads of beautiful women in and out of here, a lot of them actresses and celebrities. Besides, Frank's handy if I need a chaperon."

"Well, have you met any eligible men there?" Tom joined in. "How about a good-looking actor?"

For a moment Sheri thought Frank might have blabbed about Race Evans, but she shook the notion aside. If he had, her brothers would have already given it away. She had to smile at Tom's misdirected concern for her social agenda. "I'm not interested in having a man in my life right now."

"Are you ever going to be interested, Sheri? You're not like Mom. Stop being afraid that you are." Now it was Doug again.

"I'm not afraid," Sheri said, knowing that her answer probably wasn't true. Their mother, Rita, had been married five times—first to Tom and Doug's father, and following the divorce, to Sheri's dad. A Houston policeman, Bob Lindsey was killed thwarting an armed robbery when Sheri was thirteen. After that, it seemed to Sheri there was a revolving door of stepfathers. It had been impossible to convince her mother that another kind of life was possible. "What can I do, honey? The only thing I know is cooking, sewing and keeping a home."

When Sheri had suggested Rita get a job or go back to school, she was firmly told, "But I like being a housewife and having a husband." Finally Sheri had accepted the fact that Rita was one of those women who felt she had to have a man taking care of her. Too bad her overdependent attitude kept running them off. And in the process scaring her daughter about marriage and commitment.

"I'm not afraid," she reiterated to her brother.

"I hope not, because marriage can be pretty great if you find the right person, although I have to admit that my fiasco with Claudia almost made me swear off relationships."

Business talk was set aside and Doug launched into a story about his former girlfriend. "Even after I tried to end it, she kept phoning, sometimes hanging up on me, sometimes just breathing. Remember, my getting an unlisted number was the only way I could stop her from calling?"

"Right. I'd forgotten about her. But tell me about your latest flame."

Doug talked enthusiastically about this new subject, and an amused Sheri sat back to listen.

CHAPTER SIX

MANNING CALLED EVERYONE together Sunday evening to brief them on the white-water excursion. Sheri, perched on an arm of the sofa, listened attentively. Her self-directed swimming therapy, coupled with her excitement about the proposed survival training, helped her view the trip in a new light. While not completely enthusiastic, she was interested. She wanted to know as much as possible about Manning's outdoor adventures; this would allow her to develop a curriculum covering every situation Wallace Security might encounter with any client—even one as unpredictable as Manning Chandler.

"We'll stick to a couple of rafts and some professional oarsmen this time out," Manning said. "No need for unnecessary risks. The Rio Chama's water level stays fairly consistent, so I think it's a good place to start. Later on, when everyone's experienced, we might take on the Rio Grande. It's more dangerous since it's undammed. That makes the water level unpredictable and harder to read."

"What do you mean 'harder to read'?" Frank looked perplexed.

"Figuring out how the water flows, knowing how it's going to react around the rocks. What you want to do is ride the line of the current. That's where the rapids are the most exciting. The guides will watch the conditions this trip.''

"What kind of clothes do we need?" Sheri asked.

"Comfortable ones. Shorts or swimsuits. Some soft-soled shoes, a shirt or sweater. A hat, sunscreen and sunglasses." Briskly he listed the items. "You'll also want to take a warm jacket, because the evenings get cool and we'll be staying overnight. Remember to pack light, though. Everything has to fit in the rafts. In waterproof bags," he added. "Okay, let's break up and get packing. We'll leave right after an early breakfast. Set your alarms for five."

Sheri lingered as the others trailed out. She wanted to tell Manning she'd again hired a helicopter for extra security. The phone rang before she could speak. Cupping his hand over the mouthpiece, Manning signaled for her to stay.

It soon became clear that his caller was the mysterious correspondent. This was a new development, and Sheri was glad she'd insisted every call be recorded. She moved closer, anxious to hear what was being said.

"What have you got against me, buddy?" Manning frowned. He stretched, then massaged the back of his neck with his free hand. He paced, pulling the phone cord to its full length. Sheri shadowed him, while trying to keep out of his way. "Listen, why don't we meet and talk about whatever's troubling you? Maybe we could work something out."

Manning's agitation increased during the few minutes he was on the phone. The caller was doing most of the talking, allowing Manning only a sentence or two. "Your argument is with me. Don't take any chances on hurting someone else..."

As the conversation ended, Manning's shoulders sagged. He slumped into the swivel chair behind his desk and rested his elbows on the desktop.

"Did you recognize the voice?"

"No."

Sheri hit the playback switch on the recorder. She couldn't place the caller, either, couldn't even tell whether the voice was male or female. But she sensed something familiar, though she couldn't identify what. She played the message again. The words were gravelly, the person obviously camouflaging his natural voice.

"It seems muffled, as if he had cotton stuffed in his mouth. But the warning's explicit enough—an accident will happen tomorrow." Manning jerked his thumb toward his chest. "Apparently I'm to come back from the trip in a body bag."

"We're not going on any trip!" Sheri was adamant. "This is too much. You can't insist on flaunting yourself in view of this."

"Of course we're not going," Manning said, his voice tinged with frustrated anger. "I'm not stupid. I may want to take the battle to him, but I'm not about to risk anyone else's life in the process. That phone call convinced me the guy's probably serious."

"We have to discuss what to do next. I think we should call in the police."

"No, not yet. I still want to avoid publicity if I can. Call Anson and have him send some more of your people up here. I don't want anyone to know who they are—*I* don't even need to know. If this fool's planning to come out in the open, we're going to be ready.''

SECURITY PROCEDURES changed as a result of the latest threat. One agent spent nights in a chair outside Manning's bedroom door. Other agents accompanied him every single moment, from the house to the fitness center and from the center back to the house. As instructed, the Albuquerque office had sent in reinforcements.

Manning's staff members also became involved, scrutinizing all delivery and service people and watching the comings and goings of guests. But it wasn't long before everyone, staff and security agents alike, had become restive and weary from the increased surveillance—and from Manning Chandler's renewed belligerence. The enforced restrictions on his activities were obviously frustrating him. "About the only place I get to be alone is the bathroom," he grumbled.

"And that's only because we've sealed the window," Frank countered.

As the week passed, Manning's temper flared more and more often. The considerate and caring man Sheri had come to know barked out orders and snapped at anyone who questioned them. "Bring the car around. *Now!*" he bellowed at Frank one morning.

"Well, what are you standing there for?" he continued to shout. "Is that request too complicated for you? I'm going to be late if you don't get cracking." Manning was a few minutes behind his scheduled de-

parture for Santa Fe where he had an appointment
with the CEO of a major hotel chain. The agents knew
he was a stickler for punctuality, but this was the first
time they'd witnessed a tantrum over a mere five minutes.

The meeting ended at about three and, according to
Frank, the trip there and back passed silently, with
Manning staring morosely out the car window.

Angela, who'd returned to the spa with some of the
film people, was the next unsuspecting victim of
Manning's tongue. She walked in on a business session of the Fort staff, and Manning demanded she
leave.

"Well, excuse me," she said huffily, turning on her
heel and stomping back through the open door.

Even Cookie and Juan weren't exempt—Cookie
was chastised for serving a cholesterol-laden meal, and
Juan for talking too long on the telephone with his
girlfriend.

Immediately after dinner that same day, Manning
rose from his seat and strode off to the patio where he
slouched in a lawn chair and gazed into the night.
Several agents sat across the pool guarding him, but
wary of getting close to their unhappy client. The skies
had darkened, and a full moon hung overhead when
Sheri ventured outside to bring him news of another
threatening note.

She had no idea what to expect but was prepared to
beat a hasty retreat if he yelled at her. He paid no attention as she stood watching him, her fingers curled
around the redwood frame of a chair beside his. She

had to clear her throat before he acknowledged her presence.

"What do you need?" he growled. Manning looked tired. His usually immaculate appearance was marred by his rumpled hair and the faint trace of a beard that shadowed his jaw.

"Are you all right? Is there something I can do?" She came around the chair to face him.

He shrugged. "I've just been wondering how long this can continue. I feel like I'm under siege. We're going to lose the hotel contract. They heard rumors about the situation here and asked for that meeting. After I gave them the details this afternoon, they said they couldn't sign. If the problem isn't cleared up within the week, they'll approach someone else. The CEO said he couldn't afford the risk."

"I'm sorry," Sheri said. "This is really bothering you, isn't it?"

"Of course." He gave her an incredulous stare as if he couldn't believe his ears. "The Fort's my dream come true. If I lose this deal, it's likely to have a domino effect. How would you feel if your company was in danger of going down the drain?"

"You've got a point, but—"

He held up a hand to halt Sheri's words. "You think this is just a toy for me? That because I've got family money, I can simply go back, follow in the footsteps of my parents? Perhaps be an officer in one of their companies, chasing the buck? Well, lady, I don't want that. Money isn't what brings happiness—it's the quality of life that counts. Have a seat, and I'll share a few facts about being an heir apparent."

As Sheri sat in the chair next to his, he began his story. His parents had divorced when he was a child, and he'd remained in Houston with his father, feeling abandoned by his mother who commuted frequently to New York City for her company and couldn't have her son with her.

Sheri knew that his mother was as successful as his father. Esmee Fontenant had inherited a small but prestigious cosmetics company from her family and transformed it into a worldwide enterprise. Manning Chandler was one of those fortunate people born with *two* silver spoons in his mouth. The drawback of being the son of rich ambitious parents, however, was that they rarely had time for him.

"As you know, I gave Chandler Oil a try. But nobody—except a few people here at the Fort, and maybe my father—knew how much I hated it. I started biding my time...searching for options."

"And how did you hit upon a spa?"

"Dumb luck. I was looking around for a commercial venture. On a ski trip, I happened to hear this place was for sale. Physical fitness has always been an interest of mine. I decided to combine that with a business and bought it the next day.

"I was willing to invest my entire trust fund in the purchase. It was worth the money just to secure my freedom. Both my parents wanted to help, but it was important that I do it on my own—so to speak, considering the trust. But if the Fort fails, I'll have to go back to some kind of corporate job, or end up as a ski bum—the hedonistic life-of-the-party type you've always seen me to be."

"What I see tonight is someone with a bad case of 'poor me,'" Sheri said. "At least you had some choices. Not everyone does. Sure you've got a problem right now, but that doesn't mean you have the right to be a bear and take it out on everyone else. It's beneath you."

"Oh, Sheri, you do force me to toe the line. Always making it very clear what you think of me. And you pull away like a frightened rabbit every time I get too close."

Sheri refused to respond to his last statement. "Let's return to the problem at hand."

He smiled ruefully. "And your solution?"

"Be patient a little longer. Anson and I think our guy will come out into the open within a few days. He's increasing his contacts with the Fort. Juan brought me another letter only a few minutes ago. It'll be over soon."

"I hope so," Manning groaned. "I really hope so." He shook his head. "Everyone thinks I've been a bear recently?"

"A grizzly. Didn't you notice the wide berth those guys are giving you?" Sheri gestured toward the agents, then smiled to show she was only half-serious. "According to Anson, they're trying to avoid your claws."

"I guess I'd better apologize to the lot of you. By the way, it's good to have Anson back." Manning managed a chuckle. "I noticed him leaving one of the cabanas in his flowered Bermuda shorts pretending to be a guest. But I don't think he fooled anyone. The black socks probably gave him away."

Sheri laughed at that. Anson undercover at a ritzy spa was as likely as a hound trying to pass for a poodle. But she realized Manning had found another problem with Wallace. The training needed to include effective strategies for working undercover. "Well, I think I'll turn in. Good night, Manning."

"Good night," he answered softly. "And, Sheri," he called after her, "be careful. One of these days the rabbit might get caught in my snare."

IT WAS FRIDAY EVENING, and Sheri was sitting in a straight-backed chair in Manning's office, dividing her attention between the spy novel on her lap and the flip chart Manning was working on.

"I promised to do a presentation for a Boy Scout Jamboree in Taos," he explained. "I'm determined, so no arguments. Thought I'd talk a little about nutrition, then about how the various muscle groups interact." He was sketching a biceps when Sheri was startled by a loud voice shouting, "Shoot! Shoot!"

She was off her chair—her book flying under the desk and the chart tumbling into a corner—and had Manning on the floor out of harm's way in seconds. Manning was beneath her, at first still, and then trembling. But it wasn't from fear, she suddenly realized, it was laughter. Manning's body vibrated as he rolled her over, pinning her down with his weight. He continued chuckling.

Sheri again heard "Shoot!" but this time she could tell that it was coming from the basketball court across the driveway. Her face reddened.

"I said you guys are overzealous," Manning chastised, "You in particular, Sheri—maybe because you read that crime stuff, instead of those romances I gave you." He pulled her spy novel from under the desk, scanned the cover and shook his head before tossing the book aside.

"Still, it's nice to know I'm safe and sound. Good moves, Lindsey." With his body pressed so close to hers, Sheri swore she could feel his every muscle, and her pulse quickened in response. She tried to twist away, but he wouldn't let her go. Despite her conditioning, Sheri was no match for his superior strength.

Manning's laughter had stopped now, and he was gazing down at her, his eyes caressing her. After long moments, his head lowered, his lips joined hers, and all thoughts of protection vanished from her mind.

This kiss was different from the one in the pool. That one had been short-lived and gentle. This kiss was potent—full of primal hunger and determination. When he finally eased his lips from hers and looked searchingly into her face, she was too overcome to do anything more than stare weakly back.

Suddenly the office door opened, revealing Juan and Frank standing on the threshold, mouths agape. Sheri's dark eyes rounded in embarrassment as she realized how this little display of togetherness must appear to the men.

Manning quickly shifted to a sitting position. "Come on in, guys," he said. "You've got to hear this." Then he started chuckling again as he related Sheri's "daring" rescue. He turned to Sheri. "I'm impressed by your diligence, Agent Lindsey, but I think you can relax. I doubt that getting beaned by a basketball would do me much harm." He laughed even louder, and Juan and Frank joined in.

Sheri was fuming. She saw nothing *that* funny in the situation. She'd simply been doing her duty, something any professional would have done. And look where it had landed her. First, an accidental embrace—from which her racing pulse was just beginning to recover—then ending up the fall guy in an exaggerated account of the whole ridiculous scene. Nothing could be more humiliating—except to have Manning accuse her of staging the rescue to make a pass at him.

She got to her feet and straightened her clothing. "If I've provided enough amusement for everybody," she said with all the dignity she could muster, "then I think I'll take a break." She left the office, scowling at the sound of the guffaws that followed her down the hall.

In the solitude of her bedroom, Sheri could still feel the unsteady beat of her heart. Ever since Manning's negative reaction to their encounter in the swimming pool, she'd dared not expect any more kisses. More than once, she'd longed for his kiss, had dreamed about it. But not like this. Not with him laughing as if it was nothing but a big school-yard joke.

Sheri felt an inexplicable desire to cry. A few tears seeped from the corners of her eyes before she managed to control herself. She'd always prided herself on being the opposite of a high-strung weepy female. However, her experience with Manning Chandler made her realize that she'd probably been unfair to those women she'd always disdained for giving vent to their emotions. Another tear rolled down her cheek. Finally she succumbed to her feelings and fell across her bed, crying unashamedly.

"COME ON, SHERI. You can't pretend it didn't happen." It had been two days since the embarrassing incident, and Manning had intercepted her in the hallway outside her bedroom.

"I most certainly can," Sheri assured him. "And that's precisely what I intend to do." She wondered why he was in the agents' wing. It had become her retreat when she wasn't on duty, mainly because Manning never bothered to venture there.

He fiddled with the collar of her blouse as he spoke. "You've got to stop hiding from me. We both know why it happened."

"If you're trying to say I intentionally prompted it, then you're wrong. I'm sick to death of your inflated ego. Not every woman collapses in a heap simply because you throw a couple of kisses her way. Now, can we just forget the whole thing?" she muttered, stepping back from his touch.

"I'm making no such accusation. That kiss was inevitable, and frankly *I'm* finding it rather difficult to forget." Manning's lips curved in a teasing grin.

"Small wonder. You had a good chuckle at my expense, didn't you?" Sheri's indignation was rising in direct response to the attraction she was feeling. Damn him. Despite his irritatingly smug attitude, he *was* attractive. No wonder Angela and those other women were desperately chasing him.

"Is that why you're so angry? What did you expect me to do—tell the truth? After all, we were caught in a rather compromising position. I thought you'd prefer having everyone laugh about it, instead of suspecting what really happened."

Sheri paused, not knowing what to say. He was right, of course. It would have been more than embarrassing if the other agents had known the complete story. Still, the laughter was almost as unbearable. Juan and Frank had been heckling her ever since their ill-timed entry. Even Cookie, who rarely cracked a smile, had been unable to resist joining in the banter.

She was often accused of possessing too serious a nature, but Sheri usually managed to take teasing in stride. This particular incident, though, was testing her patience. Perhaps because the emotions that had surfaced were in no way amusing. Everything now seemed more complicated because of that unexpected kiss. Yet she couldn't fault Manning's logic. If there was a choice between embarrassing and unseemly, she'd opt for the former. "Okay, I see your point," she agreed reluctantly.

"Friends again?"

Sheri hesitated and looked at him, her eyes questioning. *When had they been friends?*

"Please?" He flashed her another of his devastating smiles, and Sheri was lost.

"Friends. As long as I don't have to hear one more word about that episode."

"Not a word. At least not from me. I've got to stay in your good graces. The next time you hear 'shoot' you may decide 'good riddance to him,' and with my luck it would be the real thing. No, I want you on my side." He winked. "See you later, lovely Sheri."

Sheri returned to her bedroom and glanced at herself in the mirror. She could see a flush in her cheeks, a flush that hadn't been there a few minutes earlier. The turmoil of the past few days was behind her, and she suddenly felt better. In fact, she felt wonderful. All because...all because Manning had called her "lovely Sheri" again. Or was it because of what he'd said about not forgetting their kiss? Could it really have been that memorable for him, too? She sighed, wondering how she was going to act like a professional during the rest of this detail—and what was going to happen once it was over.

Sheri had no idea the situation would be resolved that very afternoon. She freshened her makeup and went downstairs, settling into a chair outside Manning's office, watching a stream of staff and guests come and go. Manning had always maintained an open-door policy, and a trail of people was not unusual. Most of the guests who dropped in to the office had close ties with the Fort and with him.

So far there was nothing out of the ordinary, including another one of Angela's frequent visits. As Angela passed by, Sheri felt a spurt of annoyance at the woman's total lack of subtlety. In pursuing Manning, Angela was as persistent as a fly at a picnic—and about as welcome. She seemed almost obsessed with him.

As she sat there and reflected, Sheri began to feel uneasy. Something niggled at the back of her mind.

She tried vainly to figure out what was bothering her. It was like knowing the lyrics to an old song, but not being able to remember them. There was some connection to her brother, Doug. But what was it?

Sheri rose to her feet and stood in front of the office door, putting her ear against it to listen to the conversation. She might be guilty of blatant bad manners, but a sixth sense told her to proceed.

"I've done everything I know to get you to return my love, Manning," Angela was saying. "I've cooked, I've tried to fit into your life-style. Yet you treat me like your kid sister. I was hoping you'd turn to me if you felt there was a problem, that you'd confide in me, but all the notes accomplished was to occasionally distract you from other women. But at least that was something. Then you called *her* in."

Angela! How could I have been so dense? Sheri wondered. Wallace was dealing with a man constantly surrounded by women—why had they been so certain the culprit was a male? A female made just as much sense. Sheri shivered, then eased the door open. Now she remembered Doug's telling her about some of his old girlfriend's behavior, about how she wouldn't leave him alone. But Doug had shared that tale with her weeks ago—why hadn't she made the connection earlier?

"Well, here's the lady in question now," Angela drawled as she glared at Sheri who stood in the doorway.

Manning tried to move toward Sheri, but was restrained by the flick of a well-manicured hand, a hand that held a thirty-eight revolver, a trembling hand.

Sheri was afraid Angela would pull the trigger from pure nervousness. People holding guns often did.

Angela jerked her head at Sheri. "Ever since she's been here, you've excluded me from everything. Once, you'd have taken *me* rafting." She pointed the gun at Manning's chest. "If I can't have you, nobody can."

"But the voice on the telephone . . ." Sheri had to divert Angela's attention, had to keep her talking and buy some time. She dared not draw her own gun while Angela had Manning in her sights. "Who else is involved in this?" She struggled to keep her words calm and even.

"No one else. Just me." Angela cackled loudly.

"The voice on the telephone," Manning said, echoing Sheri. "It was a guy." Sheri could sense no trace of fear in him and was amazed he had such control.

"You'll come home in a body bag," Angela responded in a low gravelly voice, the voice on the tape. "Actually—" she trained the gun on Sheri "—you're the one I'd prefer to see in a body bag."

The split-second twist of Angela's body gave Manning the opening Sheri had been hoping for. His quick blow to Angela's wrist sent the firearm sailing across the room. Sheri dived after it, grabbed it, then rolled to her feet. She removed the bullets and tossed the weapon aside. Guns were no longer needed. Manning was already leading a hysterical Angela to the sofa, and Frank, Anson and Juan were at the door, summoned by the noise.

"What's going on?" they asked in unison.

"Meet our pen pal." Sheri gestured toward Angela.

"Well, I'll be damned," Frank said. "I guess I'd better call in the police."

"No!" Manning ordered. "No." He glanced at Sheri for understanding. "I think what we really need is medical attention." Angela sat sobbing on the sofa, her head buried in her hands.

"But..." Sheri wanted the woman locked up and as far away from Manning Chandler as possible, yet it was clear Manning wouldn't change his mind.

"Anson, will you handle this?" she asked. "Get her to the infirmary, then make some phone calls and see where she can be placed. Get in touch with the film people, so they can contact her family." Sheri was amazed she could manage the instructions. Her heartbeat was still erratic, and a glance at her hands confirmed they were now shaking as much as Angela's had. But it was over. *Over,* she repeated to herself. She looked at Manning.

In return, he smiled and mouthed a silent thanks before directing his remarks to Anson. "I want her to have treatment, but I don't want the police brought in. If we involve the law, it'll destroy her."

"Chandler, the woman might have killed you," Anson said.

"I don't think so. She had her chance before Sheri came in, and she didn't take it. Angela's not a real criminal. She just has more problems than anyone realized. None of us took her seriously. Now, let's make up for it and take care of her. And I'm not being totally altruistic. I don't want any bad publicity if we can avoid it, and I think we can."

By midnight, Anson had arranged for Angela's admittance to a private hospital in Albuquerque. Later, she'd be transferred to southeast Texas to be near her family.

After the realization had sunk in that the crisis was indeed over, the Wallace Security and Fort Tranquillity staffs were in a festive mood. Sheri shared a glass of champagne with the group, then retreated to her room, grateful that, with the investigation at an end, she had no shift tonight. She was exhausted, ready to drop into bed. But more than that, she was disappointed in herself. She needed time to deal with her failure to solve the mystery.

She had already changed into her pink-and-white striped pajamas and a cotton robe before realizing that she'd left her novel in Manning's office. She was going to retrieve it when she saw Manning coming up the stairs. She met him on the landing and stopped him.

"I didn't want to interrupt the celebration, but I'd like to talk to you."

"Anytime." Manning followed her into his office and rested a hip on the edge of the desk.

"Wallace Security owes you an apology. It appears your concerns about our abilities were well-founded. That scenario with Angela should have been headed off."

"It was headed off. You looked beautiful coming through that door—like an avenging angel."

"Belatedly. I missed all the clues."

"There weren't many. Besides, everyone underestimated Angela."

"But *I'm* not supposed to make that kind of mistake."

"No." He moved toward Sheri. "You're supposed to be perfect. That's the standard you set for yourself, isn't it? Well, you're not perfect." He smiled. "But close enough. Cut yourself a little slack, Sheri. It's finished, and you can relax now."

Obviously Manning Chandler held no grudge against Wallace Security. And everything *had* turned out all right—probably even for Angela. Maybe Sheri did need to tone down those exacting standards she'd set for herself.

"Are you through pondering what I said?"

Sheri nodded. "How did you know I was 'pondering'?"

"Because I know you," he said, caressing her cheek. "Now how about a celebration kiss?"

"You've had too many glasses of bubbly." Sheri backed away, almost touching the wall. She might have decided to forgive her own lack of professionalism, but she wasn't about to forget the reason for her lapse.

"Only one glass. I don't need alcohol. I'm high on happiness. So, how about that kiss?" He placed his two hands against the wall on either side of her, effectively capturing her. Sheri searched for a way out.

"You get very jittery when I come near," he said. "It makes me wonder... How many times have you been kissed, anyway? Apparently not often enough."

Sheri stared into his eyes, forcing herself not to melt in their warmth, not to react to his seductive words. Because Manning was too good with words, and she'd seen him charm the women visiting the Fort. Now, in his relief, he seemed intent on pursuing her. For him, it was only good-natured teasing, but Sheri knew her feelings went deeper. She couldn't risk becoming any more involved than she already was.

Sheri tried pushing him away, with little success. "My kissing experience is not your concern."

"Sweet—what?—twenty-seven? And never been kissed," he persisted.

"Twenty-eight. *And* I've been kissed."

"I meant by anyone before me."

Sheri's brown eyes narrowed as she looked up at him. "I thought we'd agreed to forget that last unfortunate incident."

"Forget it? Uh-uh. I agreed not to say anything to anyone else. But I didn't agree to amnesia." He slid his hand down the wall and onto her shoulder. "Actually, if the truth be known, I'd like to repeat it."

"Not a chance," Sheri said, ducking under his other arm and escaping out the door. She'd forgotten her book, after all.

SHERI STAYED AWAKE most of the night attempting to put her feelings in perspective. She'd cautioned herself a thousand times, but despite that, she was starting to care too much. She'd allowed her emotions to interfere with her professionalism. Try as she might to excuse herself, she couldn't ignore the fact that she'd made a serious mistake, a mistake that could have cost a life—Manning's life.

A wave of depression overtook her. How had she managed to be so foolish? She couldn't ever let such a thing happen again. A cardinal rule at Wallace—and her personal rule, too—was, "Don't get involved with the clients." Well, for the balance of this assignment she'd keep Manning Chandler at arm's length. And for as long as she was a security agent, she'd remember to stay uninvolved.

Remaining aloof proved impossible, however. Sheri and a group of agents stayed on to complete the terms of the security contract. At this point, it was difficult to remember the adversarial relationship the Wallace staff had once had with Manning Chandler. His playful and charming mood bore little resemblance to his former attitude, and the good cheer was infectious.

His high spirits intensified after a successful business meeting in Santa Fe with the hotel CEO who'd now decided to sign the contract and send his international executive staff to Fort Tranquillity for a series of week-long retreats. It would be the Fort's largest contract to date, and Manning was throwing a party by the pool to celebrate.

The film crew had returned, too, but since this was their last day in New Mexico, the party became a farewell. Sheri was pleased that she'd had a chance to slip into Santa Fe to purchase a sundress, a splashy red floral with straps that crisscrossed her back. She was also pleased that her job kept her in shape, because the dress revealed a lot of neck, shoulders and leg—much more than her usual slacks and cotton shirts did.

A three-piece band was setting up by the cabana when Sheri appeared. Juan, who had put together this impromptu party, had done a masterful job. The patio was decorated with colorful balloons, flowers and streamers. He was supervising the caterer's staff when Sheri walked up to survey the buffet table, a Mexican feast of guacamole, miniature tacos and chalupas, bowls of red and green salsa, salad, tamales, enchiladas, tostados, posole and chiles.

She took a diet cola from the bar and sat down at a poolside table. Manning and Race Evans soon joined her. Manning was wearing a tan sport coat, tan slacks and a teal shirt that made his eyes seem even bluer. Sheri hoped he didn't realize the effect those eyes had on her. At the moment, she was feeling as tongue-tied as an adolescent on her first date. It occurred to her that she hadn't even noticed what Race was wearing. The oversight, had he known of it, would clearly have astonished the popular actor, accustomed as he was to female attention.

"Angela . . ." Race's voice trailed off. "Who would have guessed that someone with the film was causing all your trouble? But she *was* taken with you, Manning. She even boasted to one of the other actresses that she was going to marry you. Her crush goes back a long way, too. She grew up near Houston and started a scrapbook about you the year the newspaper named you one of the city's most eligible bachelors. She showed it to a couple of the girls, and they told me."

"I had no idea," Manning said. "Of course, I always assumed it was a man harassing me, and I could have sworn it was a man on the phone. I listened to the recording this morning and heard the voice with my own ears, but I still have difficulty believing it was her.''

''She *is* an actress. And she has a natural talent for mimicry—male, female, any dialect. I thought she might really go places because of that.''

''I remember now,'' Manning said. ''One night she did impressions for us. An Irish brogue, an Eliza Doolittle cockney number. It just didn't occur to me....''

''Nor to me,'' Sheri added. She saw no point in acknowledging that her personal feelings had clouded her vision. She'd disliked Angela from the first, but hadn't considered that she could be involved in the case. Despite checking out the film people along with the other guests, Wallace Security had failed in this instance. It was never going to happen again, she reminded herself. Next time, she'd suspect everyone—maybe even their own agents—until she had proof to the contrary.

Sheri was enthralled by Manning's upbeat mood. Although initially surmising that his spa business was just a rich man's plaything, she'd come to understand how important the Fort was to him. It wasn't merely a temporary diversion; Manning was committed to achieving something on his own and genuinely elated about the new contract.

Surprisingly he demonstrated little concern that the bevy of beauties was leaving. She'd been observing him all evening, and she'd expected that Kimberly's departure, in particular, might trouble him, but he gave no indication that it mattered. He joked, told stories and managed to dance with many of the women, Kimberly no more often than the others. Then he sought out Sheri. She and Anson were at one end of the patio, the rest of the detail at the opposite end. When Manning asked her to dance, Sheri declined. "I'm on duty," she said, determined not to forget her place this time.

"Then you need to stay close to me," he insisted.

"I need to do my job."

"The job's done. Now we can concentrate on getting the training program going." Manning took her hand and tugged her toward the dance floor. Sheri reluctantly let herself be led, deciding it was better to endure a dance than to make a scene. "You look very beautiful tonight," he said quietly.

Sheri couldn't repress a tiny rush of pleasure. If truth be told, she'd gone to special pains to wear something he'd like. And obviously she'd succeeded.

Manning kept her in his arms for a second dance. Sheri knew her colleagues and Manning's staff would be watching.

"Will you relax?" he growled under his breath.

"How can I?" she whispered back. "Everyone's staring at us."

"You're too concerned with what other people think."

"And you're not concerned enough."

"We'll talk business then." Manning eased away from her a bit, but continued turning her around the dance floor. "Since the threats are no longer a worry, how about rescheduling the rafting trip? Are you up to it?"

"Water's no problem anymore. I've been swimming every day."

"Yes, I've noticed—always with a chaperon around."

"Just following your instructions. You're the one who arranged them in the first place. You told me never to swim alone, remember?"

"Yes, but that was then and this is now. *I* could keep you company. But, then again, you've probably sought out the chaperons to prevent that. You can't avoid me forever, Sheri."

"I thought we were going to talk business." She tried to break free of his embrace. "If you want to flirt, Kimberly or one of the other women would be more amenable, I'm sure."

"I'm not interested in Kimberly or any of the others."

He hadn't released her, and Sheri was afraid to struggle anymore. She had the distinct impression that all eyes were glued on her and Manning. The second song had ended and another began immediately.

"What about the training? Are you going to leave it up to me," he asked, "or does Wallace have something specific in mind?"

Sheri was grateful he'd returned to a subject she felt comfortable with. "Maybe we could run through the type of exercise program you think we need. Then we'll expand from there." The music finally ended and Manning escorted her to a poolside table. "My brothers want to be able to handle large-scale rescue operations," she continued, looking up at him. "So, mountain climbing and rappelling should be included. Perhaps even some rafting—certainly something to do with water.''

"Do you think Wallace can manage that?"

"After a while. This is a new area for both your company and mine, and I'm sure it'll take some trial runs to get it right," she said.

"I feel I can provide what Wallace needs, but I'd like someone from your outfit assigned here full-time for at least a year." Without giving her a chance to respond, he rose from his chair. "Well, I suppose I'd better return to my guests. We'll talk later."

Sheri watched him thread his way through the crowd to the other side of the pool, clapping one of his guests on the shoulder, listening attentively to another, laughing, socializing. She felt an attack of possessiveness as she observed him chatting with the women and saw their responses to him. She thought about his request to have a Wallace representative stay on at the Fort. She was determined it wouldn't be her. She couldn't bear to remain in New Mexico with Manning that long.

For her own peace of mind, she had to leave as soon as possible. She hadn't come to the Fort for romance, hadn't planned on falling in love—no matter what her emotions were saying. Distance was the only treatment for her heartache. She'd just have to figure out a way to get one of her brothers to take over. It appalled her that after all these years of fighting their overprotectiveness, she wanted to hide behind it now.

CHAPTER SEVEN

SHERI HADN'T ANTICIPATED such a reluctant crew when she called the agents together for a briefing on the new training regimen. She was meeting with Frank, Anson and half a dozen other agents from the Albuquerque office.

"My brothers and I are committed to this project. Many of you had firsthand experience—" she cast a glance at Pete Garcia who'd joined the group "—with some of the problems we experienced at Fort Tranquillity. We want to ensure that such problems never happen again.

"In addition, this particular training fits in with Wallace's plans for an elite protection service. The time is right for further expansion, but we've got to guarantee that our agents won't fail." Sheri looked from face to face. "Admit it, gang, some of us have grown soft. In order to make this venture work we all have to toughen up, so I'd like your cooperation."

"I don't mean to be uncooperative," Frank said, "and Sheri, you know I'm in. Wallace Security hired me when the job market was really tight, and I owe the company. But I still have my doubts about Chandler being in control."

Everyone shared those doubts by four o'clock the next afternoon, after a day that started with calisthenics at dawn, then a three-mile run followed by a classroom lecture from Manning.

"Survival is what I'm teaching—personal survival and the survival of your clients. You're not always going to be in an office building. You might be in the Arctic or in the desert, and lives will depend on your knowing how intense cold or heat affects the body." Manning paced back and forth at the front of the room, occasionally illustrating a point on the chalkboard behind him.

"The more you exert yourself, the more heat your body produces. And the more you sweat, the more fluids you lose. You have to guard against dehydration. Alcohol and caffeine are no-no's when you're on assignment. These act as diuretics and increase dehydration. You need to be aware of these things, then you can pass the knowledge on to your clients."

"They'll really love us if we start harping on their vices," Frank grumbled.

"They'll love us if we save their lives," Mark, a recent arrival, put in.

Manning nodded. "Now, the first item on the agenda is to get rid of the excess weight—those 'love handles' around your middles. The only one who looks like she's seen the inside of a gym in six months is Sheri. You men are closer to gelatin molds than seasoned agents. So, there's going to be a change if you're selected for training. This is just a trial run, but if you're part of the cadre chosen for the program, then you might as well say goodbye to your present life-styles. Because I'll be telling you what to eat, when to eat, when to sleep and how to exercise."

"A lean, mean fightin' machine," Eric, another agent, griped. "I got out of the military because I was tired of people ordering me around."

"Well, for the next little while, consider yourself back in," Manning said. "The bunch of you claim to be in shape. Once you're finished with the Fort's program, you'll know what being in shape really means."

By the fourth day of training most of the group had reached a state of rebellion. They'd spent the morning running up and down the mountain path and now were side by side on stationary bicycles, pedaling furiously as they complained to Sheri, who was doing leg curls on the weight machine.

"You've got to talk to the guy, get him to let up. Otherwise, he's going to cause us permanent injury," Frank insisted. "I've endured a lot of rough training, but none of it prepared me for Chandler's methods. The man must have studied medieval methods of torture."

"Quit griping, Frank," Sheri said. She stopped the leg curls and moved to the treadmill. "The Wallace team needs this, and you're one of the guinea pigs."

"Experimental rats, you mean," Eric put in.

"Settle down, all of you." Sheri was beginning to realize that the problems were more than just physical. Obviously attitudes needed adjusting, too. Maybe Manning could suggest some motivational courses. She'd never caught *his* staff whimpering the way the agents were. Perhaps she should discuss it with her brothers.

Tom and Doug were coming to New Mexico in a couple of weeks to finalize the agreement between Fort Tranquillity and Wallace Security. She wanted them here sooner, but insisting they catch the next plane west would have piqued their curiosity about why she seemed so anxious to be out of here. She'd simply have to wait until they arrived, allowing her to return to Houston. Surely she could keep her distance from Manning Chandler for that long. But just now, she had to deal with her mutinous crew.

"This is only a temporary reprieve," she said, "but why don't we take the rest of the afternoon off? You guys swim, play poker, go into town. Do whatever you like."

"You forgot about the slave driver," Frank said. "Chandler won't agree to this."

"He will if I explain things."

"I believe I heard my name." Manning was standing in the doorway, giving Sheri a conspiratorial smile. She guessed he'd been right outside, listening to the entire conversation. He entered the room and leaned on the rails of Sheri's treadmill. "Well? What do you want to explain?"

"I decided we need a breather." She waited, expecting him to throw out a chiding remark.

"You're the boss," he said agreeably, his eyes meeting hers, then shifting to the group. "So, what are you all hanging around for? The lot of you had better leave before I change my mind. We'll continue this tomorrow."

Sheri moved her feet to the side panels of the treadmill and turned the switch off. When she dismounted, Manning was blocking her path. "Nowhere left to run, Ms. Lindsey."

"What do I...? I don't..." Sheri took a deep breath and tried again. "Who's running?"

Manning chuckled. "Let's go into town for lunch."

"I don't think so. I've got a ton of paperwork."

"Sheri, you have to realize that something's happening here—something that's never happened to me before. And I'm pretty sure the feelings are just as new to you."

"I don't have any feelings one way or the other."

"That may be what you try to convince yourself, but you *do*. I damn well know it, and I'll prove it." His arms shackled hers, and his lips hungrily crushed her own. It was a long devouring kiss that made Sheri feel as if the soles of her sneakers were melting. When Manning released her, she had to grab the treadmill to keep from crumpling to the floor.

She expected Manning to make some sort of comment, some gibe, but he looked as shaken by the kiss as she. He just watched her, his chest heaving under his cotton T-shirt. Finally he spoke. "I'll let you escape this afternoon. Because if I don't, we'll end up in bed together, and I know you're not ready for that. But some day, some day soon..." He kissed her again quickly, then disappeared out the door.

MANNING AND SHERI, with suggestions from Juan and Frank, had drafted a training curriculum by the time the extra agents were due to head back to Albuquerque. Including the two others in the planning sessions had achieved a dual purpose—it had prevented her from being alone with Manning and pacified Frank. Surprisingly he'd become as enthusiastic as she was about creating a top-flight corps of agents within the security firm.

Once Frank's complaining ceased, the others started to fall in line. Clearly he had been the ringleader. Now everyone seemed to be working hard, and the grumbling had been reduced to a minimum.

Manning watched with a smile of approval as the agents finished a set of warm-ups in record time and filed out for their morning jog. "They've finally come around," he said to Sheri as they stood off to one side. "I wasn't sure it would happen, but this group's beginning to forgo old habits and ideas."

"Some people are more willing than others to adapt their life-styles when the situation calls for it."

"Are you by chance implying that I don't?" He cocked an eyebrow as he spoke.

"If I recall correctly, you fought us every step of the way when we asked you to alter *your* behavior."

"Me?"

"You."

"You know what your problem is, Agent Lindsey?"

"What?"

"Your memory's too good." He gave her a quick peck on the cheek and raced off in the direction of the jogging track.

The training group dined on the patio that evening, along with several of the guests, including a Hollywood director who was filming a movie in South America the next spring. He'd expressed an interest in hiring a team of Wallace's special security agents and wanted to discuss his expectations for the trip.

Manning visited all his guests before settling in with the director for some business talk. Sheri had watched Manning "work the crowd," as she put it, while she sat with Frank and Juan, enjoying an after-dinner coffee.

Manning never stayed long with any one woman, never showed a preference. He was friends with many—one of those rare men who knew how to transcend the male-female barrier and be a buddy, a confidant. She could see how his playboy image had come into being; it was obviously a misassumption made by others that the women he was with were all lovers. *Not that it makes any difference to me,* she reminded herself.

"We'll have to start turning people away," Juan predicted to Sheri, "once word gets out about this new enterprise."

"That's what your boss tells me," Sheri said, focusing her attention on the conversation and injecting excitement into her voice.

"And we're going to celebrate with that long-delayed rafting trip." Manning pulled up a chair to join them. "I've made all the arrangements. We can leave early next week."

SHERI TRIED NOT TO THINK about the days passing. After all, she'd been telling herself she needed to get away from New Mexico, so why did she feel panicky whenever she realized just how soon that would be? Most of the agents were leaving the Fort the day they got back from the rafting trip. Before she knew it, her brothers would be here, in New Mexico, and she would be saying goodbye to Fort Tranquillity—and to Manning. She suppressed the thought, deciding it was better to concentrate on the present.

They continued with the indoor training activities and made daily hikes. Manning did his presentation for the Boy Scouts at the Jamboree in Taos, while Sheri's agents and the Fort staff prepared for the rafting trip.

Two days later, the whole group was assembled in a protected wilderness area where the air was fresh and clean, and the rush of the water could be heard in the distance.

Manning spread out a map on the hood of the Jeep and, using his index finger as a pointer, charted their course on the river. "We'll camp downriver tonight, and I've arranged for someone to meet us there in the morning and drive us back to the Fort. I figured some of you tenderfeet might balk at having to hike out." He cast a glance at Frank and chuckled.

"Any more jokes like that and I may balk at going at all," Frank said. Everyone else laughed, Sheri included.

Her laughter, however, was feigned. She was so preoccupied with Manning that she was barely conscious of the conversation. If only she weren't troubled by her silly daydreams, she could probably enjoy the outing and this last chance to be with Manning.

"It's important to know what to do in case you flip." Manning looked her way. "You probably won't flip, so don't let the notion worry you. If it does happen, though, the object is to protect your head. Keep your legs facing downstream with your knees bent a little. Have one leg up and one down so you can bounce off any rocks. If you're tumbling, then put your hands over your head. You don't want to crack your skull on a boulder. Understand?''

Everyone nodded.

"The guides will go over all this again, but you can't hear it too often. Here they come now."

The professional crew Manning had hired repeated his instructions and directed the group to the river-bank. Within an hour, the rafts were launched.

The gushing rapids had seemed so beautiful from the shore. But as Sheri, in the second boat, saw the white water approaching, a silent scream formed in her throat. Her fear surprised her, until she realized that a phobia so deeply entrenched wouldn't easily go away. She was determined, however, to fully conquer her fright. "Breathe deeply, deeply," she muttered to herself, reinforcing her resolve. She held her paddle tightly as the rubber raft began to bob vigorously in the grip of the current.

Manning twisted around in his seat to glance at her. "Okay back there?" he shouted.

She gave him a thumbs-up, hoping he couldn't read the panic in her eyes.

Manning was serving as oarsman in Sheri's craft, with one of the guides taking that duty in the other. Sheri felt more confident with Manning at the helm. Strange that she should find herself in such a situa-tion—in Manning's hands, so to speak. As a trained bodyguard, she felt as if this was almost a total role reversal.

With each bump and bounce, Sheri felt herself gripping her paddle tighter and tighter. At this rate, her fingers would soon be embedded in the wood. But after a while, the challenge of the water took hold, and she began to relax and actually enjoy the adventure of conquering a wild river.

Following a break for sandwiches and fruit on the bank, the group took to the boats once more and didn't touch land again until late afternoon.

The rafting company had furnished tents and paraphernalia for Manning and his entourage. Sheri had her own tent, since she was the only woman—apart from one of the guides, Deb, who was obviously involved with the main guide and stayed with him.

After a supper of panfried steaks, the group sat around a small camp fire. Embellished recountings of the day's adventures were shared, and the guides entertained everyone with tales of previous trips. There were jokes and laughter and old songs sung to the accompaniment of Cookie's harmonica.

Manning was particularly ebullient. Sheri knew he was a good storyteller, but he seemed to come into his own out here in the wild. The group erupted in guffaws as he described the time his father had arranged for him to go on a white-water excursion with the vice president of the United States and how secret service agents frantically tried to maintain close contact in a pursuit boat as the river kept sending them separate ways.

Finally the group dwindled as, one by one, people said good-night and drifted toward their tents.

Soon only Sheri and Manning were left, looking uncomfortably at each other as they realized they were alone by the fire.

"You were great today," Manning said softly.

"Oh, come on now." Sheri felt as awkward as an adolescent—certainly not the first time she'd felt this way in his presence. She pushed a wayward strand of hair back into her ponytail. "I was a mass of nerve endings for half the trip."

"That's what I mean." Manning reached around her to remove the rubber band confining her hair. He threaded the russet tresses through his fingers. "You were scared to death, yet you stuck it out without complaining. That takes real courage."

Sheri forced a laugh. "You almost make me feel good about being a coward."

"You're no coward, Sheri. You're one of the bravest women I've ever known. You fit in here, you know." He moved closer to her. "About the only thing you're afraid of is me." When Sheri started to draw away, he stopped her with a hand on her shoulder. "See what I mean?"

Sheri felt her pulse racing as Manning gently lifted her hair and kissed the side of her neck. She knew she should try to extricate herself from this precarious situation. But her heart and her common sense were at loggerheads. "I'm not afraid of you," she said boldly, and—surprising even herself—she wrapped her arms around Manning and kissed him fiercely on the lips.

She could feel his amazed reaction, as a chuckle sounded in his throat, then died. Steadying himself with one hand, he embraced her with the other. Somewhere in a corner of her mind Sheri knew she shouldn't have started this, knew she should stop it right now. But stronger emotions, magical emotions, pushed those cautions aside.

It wasn't just the solitude or the pine-scented air or the glittery night sky that worked their spell on her. It was Manning. All he had to do was ask, and she would be his. Heedless of their sleeping companions, she felt as though she was alone with Manning, alone in some familiar yet uncharted world.

Her heart began to pound faster as he pulled her against his hard chest and tenderly cradled her in his arms. She gazed up into his eyes and could see the dancing flames of the camp fire reflected there.

"Do you know how important you've become to me?" he whispered, kissing her ear.

"No."

"Very, very important. If my brain hadn't ceased to function, I'd tell you," he said, "but I want you so much I can't think." He kissed her again, a long demanding kiss.

The snapping of a twig brought them to the realization that they were no longer alone. They broke their embrace just in time to see Frank approaching.

"Hi," he said. "Couldn't sleep. Cookie's snoring sounds like a 747 preparing for takeoff. Though I'd just sit here a while and maybe he'd stop. No use lying awake tossing and turning, is there?"

"No," Sheri and Manning chorused unenthusiastically and exchanged knowing looks over Frank's back as he bent down to join them.

Thirty minutes later, when it became clear that Frank wasn't going to leave, Sheri got to her feet. "See you in the morning," she said to the men as she walked dejectedly to her tent.

"Good night," she heard them call out.

Sheri removed her denim shorts and flannel shirt and slipped a nightshirt over her head. She eased into her sleeping bag and stared into the darkness. Another thirty minutes passed without sleep.

With no distractions, she found it impossible to stop focusing on Manning or to erase memories of the way she felt when they'd kissed. Her convictions that she shouldn't get involved had completely evaporated. Best not to think about it, she decided. Best to get through the trip, go back to Houston and put her life in perspective. Perhaps with hundreds of miles separating her from Manning, she'd be able to return to her rational self. For now, she wished she had a book, a portable TV, anything to occupy her mind.

After a while, she gave up trying to sleep. She was sitting there in the darkness, hugging her knees, when she saw a shadow at the flap of her tent.

"I thought he'd never go away," Manning whispered as he crawled inside, a bottle of wine, a corkscrew and two plastic glasses clutched in his hands. "I've had this damn thing chilling since we docked."

"What are you doing here?" she asked.

"Sharing a nightcap with you." Manning's tone was hushed. They gave each other complicitous looks as he gingerly eased out the cork.

Sheri's breath caught at the soft pop. "This isn't a good idea."

Manning ignored her protest and poured the wine. He passed a glass to Sheri, then tapped his glass against hers. "To us," he said, downing the liquid, then he tossed the glass aside and took her hand. "I thought it was a wonderful idea. For days I've wanted to be alone with you, really alone. No, not just days..." He ran his fingers through her hair. "Weeks is more like it."

Sheri shivered, a million prickles assaulting her skin and her senses. When Manning pulled her into an embrace, she put her arms around him and forgot about the glass she was holding. Manning, too, seemed unaware of the wine that dribbled down his back and onto the sleeping bag as he caressed her and placed teasing kisses on her brow, her eyelids, her cheeks.

Impatiently Sheri released the glass and let it fall as she touched his jaw to urge his lips to hers. The kiss deepened, and her body eased down on the sleeping bag, followed by Manning's. His callused hand stroked the bare skin of her thigh, the roughness of his palm igniting a reckless abandon. For Sheri, reality had been suspended.

But after a few moments she remembered where she was and who she was kissing and what she'd been telling herself. She pushed Manning away. "We have to stop."

He grinned guiltily. "I didn't mean for this to happen, you know."

"No?" She eyed him doubtfully.

He raised himself slightly, resting his weight on one elbow. "No. Oh, I'm planning to make love to you. But this isn't the time or the place." He sat up, his forearms resting on his knees. His breathing had slowed, but wasn't yet steady. "I'd prefer somewhere without a covey of chaperons surrounding us. It wouldn't surprise me if Juan stuck his nose in here any second." He took her hand. "Lovemaking—the kind of lovemaking I have in mind—requires plenty of privacy." He kissed her quickly, then gathered the bottle, corkscrew and glasses. "Dream of me, Sheri," he said as he exited from the tent.

Sheri nestled down into the warmth of her sleeping bag and breathed in the faint acrid scent of the spilled wine. She drifted into sleep thinking of his kisses, of the passion they'd shared, the rapture she'd felt—and she dreamed of him.

The next morning Manning was more open in his attentions to her than ever before. All his actions seemed to carry his stamp of possession. At breakfast he motioned her to remain seated while he brought their food, then he sat by her side, playfully spreading a napkin across her lap and venturing to snare a sausage from her plate. Simple yet intimate gestures.

After the meal, Sheri wandered down to the riverbank. She stood staring into the churning currents and regretted that the trip was coming to an end. In the light of morning, Sheri's concerns had returned full force. Manning Chandler was not her type. He was

too handsome, he could have any woman he wanted,
he was a rich man's son—hardly the kind of man
who'd fall for Sheri Lindsey.

But deep within Sheri, a voice countered that he was
the man she loved.

Footsteps sounded on the underbrush, and she
turned to accept a fresh cup of coffee from Manning.
Steam rose from the cup, curling into the chill morning air.

"You enjoy all this, don't you?" he said. "The
outdoors, the peacefulness, being at one with nature?"

"I really do," she answered truthfully. "I never realized how much I would."

"And it suits you. There's a flush to your skin and
your eyes are glowing." He caressed the curve of her
cheek with the back of his hand.

She pulled away, pleased yet embarrassed at his
compliment, for it was Manning who had put that
glow in her eyes. "They'll see you." She nodded toward the others.

"Does that bother you?"

"I suppose it does. I don't like being the subject of
gossip or conjecture."

His gaze held hers for long moments, and she wondered whether he was going to kiss her. Despite her
preoccupation with a possible audience, her lips,
moistened by her tongue, parted slightly in anticipation.

"Keep looking at me like that, and I won't be able
to resist taking you into my arms. Then there won't be
any need for conjecture."

Sheri ducked her head, a deeper tinge of pink staining her cheeks. Manning tucked a finger under her chin, easing her head up. "I give you a rough time, don't I? Come on, let's help break camp." Her hand in his, they walked back to the site.

In no time, every trace of their encampment disappeared. Manning believed in environmental responsibility, a position shared by his staff and everyone from Wallace, especially Sheri. She experienced strong resentment and disgust whenever she saw self-serving graffiti on rocks, or careless littering of the countryside. Manning's commitment to keeping the wilderness in an unblemished state was one of the many things she admired about him, one of the things they had in common.

It often occurred to Sheri how much she and Manning were alike. Despite that assurance, however, she couldn't quell the nagging reminders of how they were different. Manning was a multimillionaire, the product of an affluent upbringing. Sheri was neither of those things, wasn't even close. And somehow their mutual love of the outdoors paled in comparison to these diverse backgrounds.

CHAPTER EIGHT

WHEN SHE SAW MANNING at breakfast the following day, he seemed to have resumed a business-only attitude, even though the Wallace agents had left. Sheri wondered if he was sending her a personal message, one that read, "Forget the romantic stuff and get back to work." She wanted to ask him, but the comings and goings around them presented no real opportunity for private conversation.

After their time together the past week, the intimacy they'd almost shared, Sheri had dared to hope for more. Now she was wondering if the forced proximity on the trip and the romantic lure of the woods had created an illusion.

In spite of Manning's flattering attentions at the camp, maybe she needed to accept the fact that she was destined to be simply a brief interlude in his life. He'd promised nothing, she reminded herself, made no commitments. It was irrational to expect them or to feel hurt when they weren't forthcoming.

Unfortunately she couldn't help herself, because Manning Chandler mattered to her. She'd grown to love him, ignoring all common sense and letting her heart rule her head. *Just like Mother did so many times*, she thought ruefully.

Not only had she allowed herself to fall in love, but she'd let it happen with someone who didn't share her feelings, her desire for a permanent relationship.

Her concerns were reinforced that very morning with the arrival of a new female on the scene. Sheri was beginning her daily run when her brothers arrived in the Fort's shuttle, accompanied by a stunning young woman. Sheri hurried over to the van just in time to see Manning shake hands with Tom and Doug, then embrace Suzanna Hayes.

Sheri recognized her immediately, her face familiar from the newspaper society pages. The Houston socialite was always fund-raising or organizing a charity ball. Sheri remembered from her research on Manning that the two had been engaged a few years ago, then had broken up.

Suzanna's silk blouse, tailored slacks and high-heeled sandals made Sheri, dressed in her running gear—new though it was—feel scruffy and outclassed. Jealousy raced through her body.

It had never occurred to her that one of Manning's old girlfriends might come to the Fort with her brothers. She was used to females arriving here; however, they were merely Manning's clients, and there was nothing personal, or at least intimate, in the relationships. But there could be no such rationale this time. Even if Suzanna was not *the* woman for him, she was one of Manning's own kind, and the contrast between the two served to point out Sheri's obvious shortcomings. Sheri cast a glance of irritation at her brothers. It wasn't their fault, but she couldn't help feeling as though she'd been betrayed by her family, especially since Doug was carrying what appeared to be Suzanna's makeup bag.

She continued toward them, greeting Tom and Doug with kisses and forcing as gracious a smile as she could muster when she was introduced to Suzanna. The other woman smiled warmly in return as she congratulated Sheri on the successful resolution of the threat and the new training proposal. Suzanna seemed to know a great deal about what had been happening at Fort Tranquillity. Despite their broken engagement, it was apparent that she and Manning kept in touch.

Suzanna turned to Manning, her light brown eyes luminous as topaz. "Can we go inside, darling? You know how the sun causes wrinkles."

Manning glanced at Sheri. He looked uncomfortable, as if unsure of himself around the two women. Did he think they were going to start a hair-pulling cat fight over him? He needn't have worried. Suzanna was totally self-possessed and seemingly unaware of any competition, while Sheri purposely choked back her pain at seeing the man she cared for with another woman. She watched as they moved up to the front door, Manning's hand resting in the curve of Suzanna's back—any embarrassment he might have had clearly forgotten. His voice displayed a husky, teasing quality as he assured Suzanna that she didn't need to fret about wrinkles.

Tom wrapped an arm around his sister's shoulder. "So, how're things?" He gave her a quick once-over. "Looks like you're in great shape. No broken bones or strained muscles."

"I keep telling you the best *man* for the job is usually a woman," Sheri said, putting on a smile and trying to ignore her hurt feelings about Manning and Suzanna. "Maybe now you'll believe me. And by the way," she added wryly, "thanks for bringing another beautiful woman along with you. As if we didn't have enough."

"You mean Suzanna? I wish we *had* brought her, but unfortunately, we only happened to be sharing the same flight from Houston to Albuquerque. Well, come on, give me a hug. I, for one, have missed you," Doug joked. "I hope you've enjoyed your holiday."

Sheri laughed and hugged him, then Tom. "Let's get a cup of coffee, and I'll share some of my ideas on training," she said with faked gaiety. "I'm anxious to get home and put them in motion."

"Doug and I have been talking about that, sis." Tom eased onto a bar stool while Sheri filled mugs from the coffee urn. Cookie was in the storeroom taking inventory. "Once we sign these contracts I've brought along—" he pointed at the briefcase on the floor by his feet "—then we really ought to have a full-time rep out here for a while. We've both agreed it's your assignment. You deserve complete control."

Sheri raised her mug to her lips, gently blowing the hot coffee. How like her brothers to think they knew best and to make that decision for her. Still, if she refused, they'd want to know why; after all, she'd argued so forcibly to come in the first place. But she certainly wouldn't be able to continue at the Fort, especially after seeing Manning with Suzanna. Her heart would surely crumble into tiny pieces if she had to stay around him, loving him when he didn't love her in return.

"I don't know what to say," she finally replied, thinking that at least she was being truthful, although she knew the two men wouldn't interpret the words literally. "But why don't we discuss it later? After we get the program established, it might be better to have Anson or someone from the Albuquerque office handle things here. For now, let's get you guys settled in. Chandler wants to meet with us this afternoon, and then we'll be driving into Santa Fe for dinner tonight to celebrate the contract."

Sheri escorted her brothers to their respective bedrooms before returning downstairs. She needed her run now more than ever, needed to work off her depression. She jogged the planned three miles, then, trying to avoid the main building for as long as possible, headed toward a bench by the trail to rest.

To her astonishment Doug was waiting there. Sheri sat down beside him.

"What gives?" he asked abruptly.

"What do you mean?"

"With all that's happening, I thought you'd be on cloud ninety-nine. Instead you act like the company's about to go bankrupt." His stare was unrelenting, questioning.

"I still don't know what you mean. I apologize if you think I'm not suitably enthusiastic."

Doug took her hand. "It's Manning Chandler, isn't it?"

"You and Tom are something else." She pulled her hand away. "If we were stranded on a deserted island, and a ship was wrecked on the sands, you two would think the sailor had come aground only to make a pass at your sister."

"Has he made a pass?"

"No!" Sheri's voice softened. "No, not really."

"Is that the problem? Would you like him to?"

Sheri sighed. "Let up, Douglas." But she knew better. She could tell by her brother's expression that he wasn't about to leave this subject alone. Once he got something into his head, it stayed there. "I might be a little attracted to him," she admitted. "Consider it a teenage crush."

"You're no longer a teenager."

"A woman in her twenties can be just as . . . foolish in matters of the heart as a sixteen-year-old. In any event, the man seems to have other interests. Have you forgotten the luscious Suzanna?"

"I haven't, but Chandler apparently has." He gestured toward a spot below them on the path, where Manning leaned against a fence post watching them. "What exactly's been going on out here?"

"Nothing's going on," Sheri said, as her gaze rested on Manning, and she wondered why he was there.

"I don't believe you." Doug gave Sheri a sly grin. "Hmm, baby sister's smitten with Wallace Security's new business partner. All this time we've been worried that you wouldn't let yourself fall in love because of Mom's problems. But I guess the right man hadn't happened along—until now."

"You're making a bit much of this."

Doug's grin broadened. "I don't think I am."

"I'm not about to get involved with Manning Chandler," Sheri protested.

"It's too late. You're already involved," Doug said. "So quit arguing about it and quit being so damned defensive. You aren't the first person to get hit by Cupid's arrow."

"You ought to know," Sheri accused. "You fall in love more often than other people change their socks." Her brother was handsome and charming, in some ways similar to Manning himself. But Doug fitted the "tall, dark and handsome" description that appealed to many women, a definite contrast to Manning's blond good looks. "Is the special lady still on the scene?"

"You know me," Doug said, "I've got a short attention span. There's no one at the moment. But we were talking about *your* love life, remember? Come on, tell brother Dougie what's up."

Sheri flung her arms into the air in a what's-the-use gesture. "Maybe I am—" she searched for the right word "—intrigued. That doesn't mean he feels the same way." She glanced Manning's way.

"Sure, he does. I can't believe you've reached the ripe old age of twenty-eight without realizing when a guy's attracted to you. The shapely Suzanna just got here, but instead of cozying up to her, he's afraid to let you out of his sight. We've been remiss in educating you about the birds and the bees."

"I took biology in high school and college," Sheri said. "But, anyway, we're not talking about your average male-female situation here. Like I've been trying to tell you, I'm not in the man's league."

"You're in anybody's league, Sheri." Doug's voice was gentle but insistent.

Sheri placed the palm of her hand on his cheek. "You're sweet sometimes, you know. But, Doug, look around the Fort. Think about the Chandler mansion in Houston. I'd never fit in. And if he *is* interested in me—"

"Trust me, he's interested."

"Don't interrupt." Sheri's smile softened the admonishment. "Even if he is, I wouldn't be comfortable with the Chandler life-style. I want to be an equal partner in a relationship. Chandler and I aren't equals. If he ever saw my bank balance, he'd probably fall over laughing."

"Money isn't everything."

"It is in the Chandler circles."

"I don't think money is what the man cares about— not in your case, anyway."

"Doug, leave it. Please."

Her brother shook his head. "Sheri, how can a woman as confident as you act like an adolescent when . . ." He took in her set expression. "Okay, little sister, no more advice. I suppose we'd better get back." He kissed her before pulling her to her feet and urging her toward their quarters. On the way, they passed Manning. "Hello, Chandler."

"Wallace, Sheri," Manning answered. "If you're settled in, shall we talk contracts?"

"Sure, I'll round up Tom, and Sheri can join us as soon as she's ready."

The group met for a couple of hours, discussing the details and signing the papers. Although the talks were fruitful, Sheri was restless, preoccupied with her feelings for Manning Chandler and her concern about the future. Doug had made it clear early on that the Wallace representative would be Sheri.

She wanted to leap across the table and throttle him for volunteering her like this, especially after their conversation. But she dared not get embroiled in a sibling free-for-all during a business meeting. She'd deal with her brother when the time was right.

The owner of Fort Tranquillity had made no response, leaving Sheri to deduce that perhaps he didn't care who the contact was, and that his principal interest was business, not personal relationships.

A GROUP OF EIGHT—Manning, Sheri, Tom, Doug, Suzanna, Frank, Cookie and Juan—left the Fort to celebrate at a new restaurant, one that specialized in traditional New Mexican fare. It was a pleasant evening. An impending rainstorm had caused the crowds of tourists to thin, and there were several empty tables in the restaurant. A fire flickered in a kiva in the middle of the room, casting shadows on the adobe walls.

Tonight Manning Chandler appeared to be in his element. He'd taken charge of the seating and, surprisingly, had arranged for Sheri to be on his left, with Tom on his right. A subdued Suzanna sat across the table between Doug and Juan. Suzanna seemed quite different than she had during lunch at the Fort, when she'd positioned herself next to Manning and proceeded to monopolize his time with tales of mutual friends in Houston.

Sheri wondered whether Suzanna and Manning had argued, and whether Manning might be using her to make Suzanna jealous. He was certainly attentive, even placing his hand over hers. Deftly she removed her hand and struck up a conversation with Cookie, determined not to let Manning bedevil her.

She couldn't help feeling that it was all an act for Suzanna's benefit. That dismal notion kept any pleasure at bay, and she felt the need to ruin his plans by ignoring him. Yet the more Sheri avoided Manning, the bolder his actions became. She had to suppress an indignant exclamation when he pressed his thigh against hers, a contact that couldn't have been accidental. The man was definitely up to no good.

Sheri was relieved when the meal finally ended. They strolled leisurely around the darkened plaza for a time, then returned to the Fort, where the party quickly disbanded. It had been a long day.

The Fort was quiet when Sheri slipped on a robe to go downstairs just before dawn. She hadn't slept at all and thought that a cup of cocoa might help her relax. Manning's behavior during dinner had confused her, and she'd lain awake in bed staring at the rough-timbered ceiling, trying to fathom the meaning of his behavior.

He'd acted not only as though he cared, but as though he wanted everyone to know it. So what was wrong with this picture? Suzanna Hayes, that was what. Manning had probably invited her to Santa Fe, become piqued at her for some reason and was now punishing her. Sheri vowed that she would not be a weapon for Manning to use in some sort of romantic vendetta against another woman.

She'd flipped on the light in the kitchen and was reaching for a cup when Manning joined her. He was dressed in the jeans and Western-styled shirt he'd worn to dinner, but now his shirtsleeves were rolled to the elbow, and he looked as if he'd been working.

"I wondered who was up and about." He watched as Sheri dumped instant hot chocolate mix into a cup, then added hot water. "I'd been hoping to get some time alone with you," he said, "but you scampered off to your bedroom as soon as we got home. Why do you keep running away from me?"

"The lady upstairs is a pretty good reason. I don't know what game you're playing, but I'm not in the mood." She picked up her cocoa and took a swallow.

"I'm not playing games with you, Sheri."

Sheri raised her eyes to the ceiling in disbelief. "Can you honestly say Suzanna isn't important to you?"

"Suzanna *is* important to me." Manning calmly made a cup of instant coffee and put it in the microwave. "We were engaged once, as you may know, but I broke it off."

"And now it's on again." Her efforts at nonchalance were thwarted as her voice broke.

"Wrong." The timer sounded, but Manning ignored it. "Occasionally Suzanna starts thinking we could work things out, and then she turns up. She called early yesterday morning to tell me she was in Albuquerque and on her way here. I tried to talk her out of it, but..." He shrugged. "Maybe I should've warned you she was coming." He leaned against the cabinet and smiled. "Actually I was kind of encouraged that her arrival upset you."

"I wasn't upset."

"My mistake," he said. "But about Suzanna—we go back a long way, since she was in diapers. She's an only child, and sometimes she needs a big brother. That's all there will ever be between us, and I think she finally realizes that.

"Once you get to know her, you'll see that Suzanna's fun and quite witty. She's a jewel of a pal, but in a lot of ways, we're complete opposites, and the things she likes, I detest. Parties, fancy clothes, the jet-set scene. What I care about, she doesn't—the outdoors, the Fort.

"After we broke up, she married some professional tennis player who turned out to be more of a tennis bum. It was over in less than six months, and she was pretty depressed for a while. She was hoping there might be another chance for us and wanted to talk about it. But I've finally convinced her that romantic involvement between us is impossible. We both want to keep our friendship intact, though. Any questions?"

"You don't owe me an explanation." Sheri couldn't help thinking that Manning was glossing over Suzanna's acceptance of friendship rather than romance. Now she wondered whether Manning had been using her to get his message through to Suzanna rather than trying to make the woman jealous.

"Really? Then why are you as taut as a bowstring?"

"I'm not..."

His lips curved in a smile of disbelief. "What am I going to do with you, Sheri Lindsey?"

Sheri sipped her cocoa, her brown eyes meeting Manning's over the rim of the cup. Then she cradled the mug between her hands. "Manning, you don't have to do anything with me, because I won't be here. I don't plan to stay on for the training."

"Who says?" He took the cup from her and set it on the counter. "What about Doug's commitment this afternoon?"

"Unfortunately he forgot to clear it with me. It's an old habit he has, a bad habit."

Manning frowned. "Considering what's happened between us, I can't believe you'd want to go. I won't accept it."

"I'm afraid you have to. A few kisses, a few embraces. That's all that's happened."

He put his hands on her shoulders. "That's all?"

"Manning..." Sheri knew she should protest, knew she was getting in over her head, but his body was so close, his after-shave so enticing. Her tongue moistened her upper lip.

"You always do that when you want to be kissed, you know."

"What?" Her voice was barely a whisper. Unconsciously her tongue touched her lips again.

"That," he answered, bending toward her. As his arms captured her, pulling her even closer, she grasped his waist. Their lips met, and Sheri knew she was lost.

After endless moments, Manning broke the kiss and looked into her eyes. "Should I go tell your brothers that my intentions are honorable?"

Sheri ignored the impulse to ask, "Are they?" and "What intentions?" Instead, she stared silently. Whatever Manning's motives, she couldn't deny her feelings for him. She loved him. Would this love be her undoing? "I'd better try to get some sleep," she croaked finally. Then she fled from the kitchen before she could change her mind.

Suzanna was leaning against Manning's chair reading a newspaper over his shoulder when Sheri entered the dining room the next morning. Doug was seated across the table, not too subtly eyeing Suzanna's cleavage.

As soon as he saw Sheri, Manning excused himself and moved to the coffee urn to pour her a cup. "Sheri and I are going into Santa Fe for the day," he announced as he sat down again. Four heads turned in unison—Tom's, Doug's, Suzanna's and Sheri's.

"I'm sure Suzanna would enjoy seeing some of the galleries there," Sheri said without missing a beat.

"And I'm sure your brother would be happy to show them to her. Wouldn't you, Doug?"

Doug cast Sheri a devious glance. "I'd be delighted. I want to pick up some artwork before I head back to Houston, anyway."

Sheri glared at Doug as though she doubted he could tell a Picasso from a Porky Pig cartoon. She was surprised that Suzanna hadn't protested. But the lady didn't appear to mind. In fact, she seemed almost pleased at the suggestion.

Sheri could think of plenty of reasons not to be alone with Manning Chandler. Why, then, did none of those reasons seem important right now? The only thing that did seem to matter was being away from this group and having the whole day with him. Alone.

"WHERE ARE WE GOING?" Sheri noticed that instead of driving south toward Santa Fe, they were headed north.

"Taos. I've been wanting to take you there, and it's only about an hour's drive." Manning rolled down the window and rested his elbow on the ledge. "Besides, I'd just as soon not run into Suzanna and your brother. I'm not in the mood for a double date."

The buildings in Taos were similar to those in Santa Fe, and the area had almost as much history. There was the Taos Pueblo built a thousand years before by the Indians, the Spanish mission constructed around 1615 and the artists' colony started in the 1920s, which linked D. H. Lawrence, Georgia O'Keefe and other art personages to New Mexico.

Manning and Sheri sat at an umbrella-covered table on the second-floor patio of a restaurant and ate fettucine Alfredo, accompanied by glasses of fruity white wine. From their vantage point they could watch the tourists in the plaza. After lunch they strolled through shops and galleries. Manning seemed intent on spoiling her. He bought Sheri two T-shirts, a soft green one covered in heart-shaped cacti and a white one with a row of red chili peppers. He purchased a black shirt, decorated with a gray coyote, for himself.

The last gallery they stopped at was getting ready to close when they entered. "Sorry," said the proprietor. "I need to shut down early. I'm going to see *A Midsummer Night's Dream.*"

Sheri's eyes widened. She'd hardly expected to find someone rushing off to a Shakespearean play in Taos.

"Southern Methodist University in Dallas brings a group of theater students out here every summer," the man explained.

Manning told him Sheri was from Texas, and she and the gallery owner chatted for a couple of minutes before Manning asked about a painting of yellow aspens they'd admired in the window. "If you have time, I'd like to buy it."

"It's one of my favorites, too. I'll lock the door and we can complete the sale."

As they left the gallery, Manning handed Sheri the painting.

She shook her head. "I can't accept. It's much too expensive."

"Be gracious, lovely Sheri," he said softly. "I bought it for you."

Sheri smiled a thank-you and took the package, confused by the gesture. Most men didn't spend that much on a casual acquaintance. But she had to remind herself that Manning might not place the same significance on the cost of gifts as she did. After all, the earrings he'd given her were expensive, too. Maybe he considered the painting a tip for her part in apprehending Angela?

"It's getting late. Shouldn't we be driving back?" she asked.

"I thought we'd stay here overnight. We haven't gone out to the Pueblo yet, and you don't want to miss that."

Although surprised, Sheri didn't argue. She didn't want to relinquish this precious time with Manning any sooner than she had to. "Then we'd better call. Everyone will wonder what happened if we don't show up."

"Sheri, we're adults. We don't have to check in like teenagers."

"Adults are responsible." She walked over to a pay phone. "I see no reason to worry anyone." She inserted coins and punched out the Fort's number.

"Juan? Sheri. Would you let everyone know we're not going to make it back tonight? See you tomorrow." She hung up the phone before Juan could get a word in.

She looked up in time to see Manning smiling at her. "You didn't say where we were."

"I didn't think that was necessary." She returned his smile.

Manning laughed and wrapped an arm around her shoulders. "We'd better find a room. The Taos Inn is across the street."

"*Two* rooms," Sheri corrected.

"Spoilsport," Manning teased. "I suppose I should consider myself fortunate that you're not sending me to another hotel." Then he laughed again.

After a quick stop at the hotel gift shop for a few toiletries, they went upstairs. Sheri wanted to freshen up before meeting him in the Adobe Bar for a margarita.

They paused in front of her room. "Well," she said, her back against the door, "see you in a few minutes." Manning braced his hand on the doorjamb and leaned toward her. "Why don't I come in?"

"I'm not sure that would be a good idea."

The fingers of his left hand caressed her cheek. "I want to kiss you. I'll settle for just one kiss, if you insist. But I want you in my arms without wondering whether someone's going to tap me on the shoulder and interrupt."

Wordlessly she gave him the key, and they entered her room, Manning shutting the door behind them with his heel. He took her in his arms and spun her around, capturing her body between him and the wall. Sheri reached for him, and their lips met hungrily. One kiss became two, then three, before they breathlessly drew apart.

"You'd better go," she gasped.

He pulled her toward the bed, pausing to ask, "You're not really going to throw me out, are you, Sheri?"

If he hadn't asked, Sheri probably wouldn't have offered any more objections. But he *had* asked, and now she had to be responsible. "Consider yourself thrown. I'll meet you in half an hour."

Manning shook his head in bemusement. "I'm going to have to do something about you, woman."

When Sheri entered the bar half an hour later, Manning was waiting, two icy green margaritas on the table in front of him. He tipped his glass to hers. *"Salud."*

Sheri echoed his toast, then forced her attention out the window to the street. A car had pulled up to the hotel, and a young man wearing a tuxedo got out, then extended a hand to his new bride, gowned in white lace and organza, with a flowered headband holding back her hair.

Manning took Sheri's hand and spoke. "If that were us, we wouldn't need two rooms."

Sheri smiled self-consciously. She was uncomfortable, not sure of what he really wanted from her. At this moment he seemed more concerned about their sleeping arrangement than anything else. Was it more than that?

Manning squeezed her hand. "I could probably locate a minister."

Sheri's eyes left the bride and groom to meet Manning's. "I had no idea you were such a romantic," she quipped, the calm in her voice belying the frenetic pounding of her heart. "Just the sight of newlyweds has got you fantasizing."

"I've been fantasizing ever since I met you, Sheri. Marry me. Marry me today."

Sheri's mouth dropped open. Could he be serious? "It's too late," she said, searching for something rational to say. "We'd need a license and all that stuff."

"The ever practical Ms. Lindsey. Does this mean if we had 'all that stuff,' you'd agree?"

"I don't know why we're having this ridiculous conversation." She nervously downed the rest of her drink.

"Is it ridiculous? Be honest, haven't you thought about marriage, too?"

"Look at us." Sheri glanced down at her blue-striped blouse and matching denim skirt. Manning wore jeans. "We're hardly prepared for a wedding. I didn't even bring a nightgown."

"That's the last thing you'd need." Manning smiled, a smile that started to crumble her defenses.

"There's no way—"

"If I can find a way, will you marry me, Sheri? Will you marry me right now? No hesitations?"

Agreeing to marry on a whim would be totally out of character for Sheri Lindsey—a woman who'd always been organized, precise and practical.

"I love you, Sheri," he said.

That did it. She didn't care anymore whether things made sense. Manning Chandler had just declared his love, and Sheri knew he was sincere. She could see it in his eyes, his expression. He *loved* her. That was enough. "I love you, too."

"And you'll marry me?" He stroked the palm of her hand. "If you want a big wedding, then I'll agree, but I meant what I said. I want to marry you now. I've waited a long time to find you, and I don't want to wait any longer. I don't want to give you a chance to change your mind." Manning sounded strangely vulnerable.

"I'm not going to change my mind. I'll marry you anytime, anywhere."

"How about here . . . and now?"

"But how could we? It's too late."

"Maybe not. We'll check—"

"Chandler! Manning Chandler!" a loud voice boomed nearby, startling Sheri and Manning. They looked up to see a middle-aged man hovering over them and a woman who was probably his wife standing a few feet away.

Manning rose from his chair. "Why, hello, Brownie. Nice to see you." He turned to Sheri. "Ms. Lindsey, Mr. Brown."

"Brownie—" the man corrected, taking Sheri's proffered hand and shaking it vigorously "—and this is my wife, Betty Jean. What are you doing in this neck of the woods? Business? Pleasure?"

"Sight-seeing," Manning answered. "Sheri's from Houston and hasn't seen much of northern New Mexico. I'm showing her around."

"Wonderful," Brownie said. "Why don't you two join us for dinner? We're planning to eat just down the street. Great restaurant, too. One of Taos's best."

"That's nice of you, Brownie, but we couldn't," Manning replied.

"'Course you could. Betty Jean and I are bored to death with each other, aren't we, hon?"

"If you say so," Betty Jean agreed with a smile.

Manning glanced at Sheri. "You and Betty Jean excuse us a minute." He pulled Brownie aside. When they returned, both men were beaming.

"Hon," Brownie thundered, "see about a suite and get some clothes and flowers and whatever else this little lady needs. We're going to have us a wedding." Brownie soundly clapped Manning on the shoulder. "Come on, boy, we gotta round up a license and a marryin' man—and some rings," Sheri heard him add as he hustled Manning out the door.

Sheri couldn't believe how much could be organized in less than two hours. But there she was, ready
to be married, wearing a white batiste patio dress. The
skirt was ankle-length and the shawl neckline left her
shoulders bare. Fresh flowers adorned her auburn hair
and the turquoise earrings Manning had bought her
dangled from her ears. Manning was still in his jeans,
but had traded his red knit pullover for a white Western shirt and bolo tie.

The suite was decorated with vases of roses, gladi-
oli and chrysanthemums, and a small wedding cake
and several bottles of champagne sat on a table in the
corner. The hotel had even rigged up a makeshift altar where Manning and the hastily acquired minister
stood waiting for her.

A classical guitarist strummed a love song as she
made her way toward the altar. It was the first time
she'd seen Manning since Brownie had stolen him
away to arrange the ceremony. Betty Jean had kept
Sheri busy, never giving her a moment to reconsider.
But even though the actual wedding, with its hurried
arrangements, was a spur-of-the-moment decision,
Sheri felt a comforting sense of certainty about being
married to Manning.

The wedding was perfect. Just what Sheri had always wanted—small and intimate and personal. Her
voice broke as she repeated her vows, and she had to
wipe a tear of joy from her cheek. Manning's voice
was husky with emotion as he slipped a gold band on
her finger and said the pledges that had endured
through time.

Brownie and Betty Jean joined them for cake and a glass of champagne. They were pleasant, gracious people, who seemed to know everyone in Taos. They'd convinced shop owners to reopen and even managed to get the necessary paperwork done. They also seemed to know when the newlyweds needed to be alone.

Sheri and Manning shared a private glass of champagne, toasting their new life together. Then they took a relaxed stroll along the quiet streets of Taos, stopping for a light meal before making their way back to the hotel. Sheri had anticipated her new husband would steer her to the bedroom once they were alone, but he surprised her. It was as though he was giving her time to adjust to what had happened.

"Brownie's quite a guy." He wrapped an arm around Sheri's waist as they walked. "He helped me by doing a rush job on the renovations when I was setting up Fort Tranquillity. Like a lot of people, he's become part of my extended family. Did you mind having a couple of strangers as our witnesses?"

"No. Besides, they were comfortable to be with. As if they were old friends." Sheri spoke the truth. Most of Manning's friends were nice. Affluent, maybe, but Sheri had to admit they didn't treat her like an outsider. It was her own defensiveness that made her stress the difference in status.

When they reached the door of the honeymoon suite, Manning picked her up and carried her over the threshold. He didn't put her down until they were inside the bedroom. Manning eased his arms from under Sheri's knees, and her feet slowly slid to the floor.

As they stood facing one another, his hands went to her waist and hers rested on his shoulders. A kiss, two kisses, then he stared happily into her eyes, whispering, "I love you, Mrs. Chandler," as he plucked the flowers from her hair.

SHERI LAY WATCHING HIM the next morning while he slept, an endearing soft snore coming from his parted lips. She felt a shudder of pleasure as she realized how all her fantasies had become real. Manning Chandler was her husband, and he loved her. She thought she would burst with joy.

He opened his eyes and saw her studying him. "What's wrong?"

"Nothing. I'm just thinking about how happy I am."

"Good." He reached for her. "Now come over here where you belong and prove it."

She moved into his arms. "I wish we didn't have to go back today."

"Me, too. But unfortunately your brothers are waiting at the Fort for a second round of planning. I can't afford to offend my new in-laws—not in the first twenty-four hours, anyway."

"Those guys have always had a knack for being around at the wrong time. Some days I think—"

Sheri was silenced by Manning's kiss, and thoughts of her brothers quickly vanished.

After a leisurely breakfast in bed, they left for the Fort. During the hour's drive back, Sheri and her new husband shared lighthearted conversation and laughter, reveling in this time that was their own. The car had no sooner stopped than Tom and Doug bounded out of the house, followed by Juan and several other staff members. It appeared that the main household had been in an uproar.

"Where were you?" Tom demanded, jerking the car door open.

"Some greeting." Sheri climbed out and gave Tom a peck on the cheek.

"Don't change the subject." Tom took her shoulders, a familiar big-brother frown on his face—the same one she'd seen the time she stayed out past three in the morning on a date during her senior year in high school. "You've been gone all night."

"Your powers of deduction amaze me," Sheri said, her temper rising like the mercury in a thermometer in August. So what if she'd been out all night with a man? So what if she'd slept with him. It was none of Tom's business. She was too old to be treated this way.

"Perhaps I'm talking to the wrong person." He released her and turned to Manning. "Where have you two been, Chandler?"

"That's none of your business." His words echoed Sheri's thoughts. Manning glanced over at Doug. "Are you involved in this lynching party, too?"

Doug grinned. "No, actually *I* was thinking more along the line of fetching my shotgun—as in shotgun wedding."

Manning laughed and pulled Sheri to him, his fingers gripping her shoulder. "You're quite right. I should do the honorable thing." A smirk played on his lips. "There's only one little problem—I'm already married."

Two pairs of brotherly eyes narrowed as both missed the mischievous glint in Manning's gaze. Manning was obviously enjoying himself, and Sheri felt like giggling at Tom's and Doug's incredulous expressions.

"The hell you say," Tom growled while Doug looked ready to start throwing punches.

"Before you boys get violent, I'll just say that Sheri and I were married yesterday in Taos." He stuck out his hand. "So, how about some congratulations for your new brother-in-law?"

Sheri could see the relief on her brothers' faces as they gave Manning enthusiastic handshakes and pats on the back. With the tension diffused, the group moved inside, where Cookie had already laid out a buffet lunch.

Her brothers tried to convince her to have another wedding—a formal affair with all the attendant hoopla, but Sheri adamantly refused. She'd consent to a party, with her family and Manning's also, but she didn't want a traditional ceremony. Her wedding had been perfect just as it was.

Sheri and Manning called their parents to share the news and invite them to a celebration at the Fort. All three seemed genuinely pleased, particularly Trey Chandler and Esmee Fontenant. Esmee welcomed her new daughter-in-law with genuine warmth, and Trey echoed Esmee's sentiments, adding that he hoped to meet her soon. Sheri was thrilled that Manning and his parents seemed ready for reconciliation, ready to become a real family.

The newlyweds spent the rest of the afternoon apart, Sheri talking to the Albuquerque office about hiring some new agents to be the first official trainees, and Manning taking Tom on a horseback ride through the hills behind the Fort to show him the entire facility. Doug had left right after lunch to drive Suzanna to the airport in Albuquerque. The evening involved a pleasant get-together around the pool with several of the spa guests.

At last Manning and Sheri were alone, walking hand in hand on the footpath. They sat on a stump, gazing at the thousands of stars in the night sky. "I couldn't believe my ears when Doug suggested a shotgun wedding," he said.

"I told you they tended to be overprotective," Sheri answered.

"I can understand that. We all love you."

"No regrets about anything, Manning?"

"What do you mean by that?"

"You know."

"I'm afraid you'll have to tell me."

"I won't be a perfect wife."

"That's a problem? I can't recall perfection being a criterion."

"I'm a disaster in the kitchen."

Manning chuckled and pulled her closer. "All the better. We have Cookie. He'll be pleased to hear he doesn't have to put up with anyone barging into his private domain."

"Sewing a button on a blouse is a major project for me," she continued. "I don't knit, crochet or do embroidery."

"I don't recall ever having any of those items on my requirement list, either."

"I like my work and I'm good at it. I don't want to quit."

"I don't want you to. You're going to be in charge of the new training program—remember? Now, have we covered all your so-called weaknesses?"

"Manning, we didn't talk about any of this before we were married. I think—"

"Hush, wife. How about letting me tell *you* what's important. I want a family...children, several of them."

"Me, too."

Manning smiled. "And I want to live the rest of my life here in New Mexico. We can travel some, see the world, but home has to be here. I want to spend most of my time in blue jeans or gym shorts. I don't care if I ever wear a tuxedo again."

"No argument there."

He took her hands in his. "Most of all, I want a wife who loves me—only me—and who wants to be with me and take care of me and let me take care of her forever."

"To love and protect?"

"That's about it," Manning said. "To love and protect, forever. Can you meet those qualifications?"

Sheri answered him with a kiss.

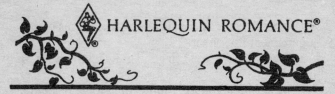

HARLEQUIN ROMANCE®

Valerie Bloomfield comes home to Orchard Valley, Oregon, for the saddest of reasons. Her father has suffered a serious heart attack, and now his three daughters are gathering at his side, praying he'll survive.

Orchard Valley

This visit home will change Valerie's life—especially when she meets Colby Winston, her father's handsome and strong-willed doctor!

"The Orchard Valley trilogy features three delightful, spirited sisters and a trio of equally fascinating men. The stories are rich with the romance, warmth of heart and humor readers expect, and invariably receive, from Debbie Macomber."

—Linda Lael Miller

Don't miss the Orchard Valley trilogy by Debbie Macomber:

VALERIE Harlequin Romance #3232 (November 1992)
STEPHANIE Harlequin Romance #3239 (December 1992)
NORAH Harlequin Romance #3244 (January 1993)

Look for the special cover flash on each book!

Available wherever Harlequin books are sold ORC-G

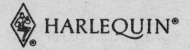